"TH[...]
FROWN[...]
THE [...]CK OPEN."

"There must be a mistake," I told Noreen. "It must be the combination to some other locker."

"I don't think so," she said quietly.

Determined now, I took the lock in both hands and turned the knob slowly and carefully. To my surprise, the door popped open as if something heaved it out at me from inside.

"I hope it doesn't do that every time I need to get it op—"

I never got to finish my sentence.

As a sickening stench washed over me, I choked and started to gag, dimly aware of someone's hands clutching my throat, clawing for air—

From far away someone called to me. . . .

I opened my mouth and heard the screams.

But not my screams . . .

Screams of pain . . . horror . . . *agony* . . .

Screams coming from my locker.

Books by Richie Tankersley Cusick

BUFFY, THE VAMPIRE SLAYER
(a novelization based on a screenplay by Joss Whedon)
THE DRIFTER
FATAL SECRETS
HELP WANTED
THE LOCKER
THE MALL
SILENT STALKER
SOMEONE AT THE DOOR
VAMPIRE

Available from ARCHWAY Paperbacks

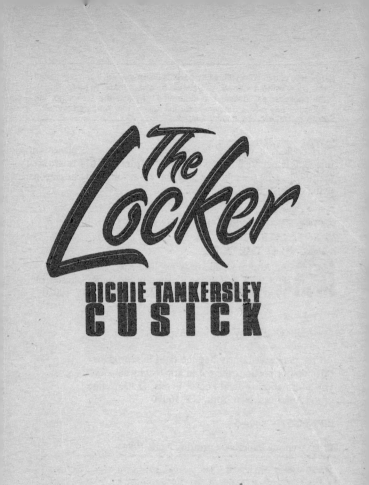

The Locker

RICHIE TANKERSLEY CUSICK

AN ARCHWAY PAPERBACK
Published by POCKET BOOKS
New York   London   Toronto   Sydney   Tokyo   Singapore

This book is a work of fiction. Names, characters, places and incidents either are products of the author's imagination or are used fictitiously. Any resemblance to actual events or locales or persons, living or dead, is entirely coincidental.

An ARCHWAY PAPERBACK *Original*

An Archway Paperback published by
POCKET BOOKS, a division of Simon & Schuster Inc.
1230 Avenue of the Americas, New York, NY 10020

Copyright © 1994 by Richie Tankersley Cusick

ISBN: 0-671-79404-3

First Archway Paperback printing April 1994

10 9 8 7 6 5 4 3

AN ARCHWAY PAPERBACK and colophon are registered trademarks of Simon & Schuster Inc.

Cover art by Gerber Studio

Printed in the U.S.A.

IL 6+

for Libby . . .

still crazy
and oh so inspiring
after all these years

1

You're looking a little strange today, Marlee," Aunt Celia said as she leaned across the front seat to shut my door. She was wearing her usual overalls with the faded red flannel shirt underneath, and her hands and cheeks were streaked with clay because she'd been up since the crack of dawn messing around with her sculptures. I'm really not sure how old Aunt Celia is—whenever I try to figure it out, I always end up somewhere between thirty and forty—but she could pass for twenty, or even nineteen, which is why everyone always wonders if she's my sister.

"What do you mean, I look strange?" I asked her, leaning back in through the open window of the van. She pursed her lips the way she always does when she's trying to avoid an issue, and then she drummed her fingers on the steering wheel.

"Your mother would—" she began, then broke off almost guiltily as I stared at her.

"My mother what?" I asked. My heart gave a painful tug, and I asked again, "Mother what?" But Aunt Celia only shook her head.

"Be careful."

Those were the last words she said to me that morning, and if I hadn't been so nervous about starting a new school, maybe I would have listened a lot more closely to what she was trying to tell me. But instead I just stood there looking up at the huge brick building with Edison High School carved over its front door. I know I should be used to brand new situations by now with all the moving around we've done, but the truth is, I still get butterflies in my stomach and wish I could be invisible. Behind me the van was sputtering dangerously as it inched away from the curb, and on an impulse I thrust my head through the window one more time and smiled down at my little brother, who was munching on a cold waffle.

"I'll come by to get you after school," I reminded him. "Be sure and tell your teacher who I am, so she won't think you're being kidnapped."

"You have to know the password," he said.

"I know it. It's Ralph."

"If you forget it, they won't let him come home with you," Aunt Celia teased. "Then he'll be stuck forever in Afternoon Adventures."

Aunt Celia's always been big on afterschool programs that enhance creativity. The one at Dobkin's kindergarten was supposed to include painting, ceramics, and how to make balloon animals.

"Don't be nervous about your new school," I added reassuringly, but Dobkin only gave me that solemn stare of his that borders on extreme annoyance.

"Are you serious?" he answered.

You have to understand about Dobkin. He doesn't have my mother's dark hair like I do, or my father's hazel eyes like I do, and the two of us aren't anything alike. When Dobkin was born, he looked so much like my maternal grandfather with his snow-white hair and huge sad eyes and really solemn face, that my parents decided to give him the honor of carrying on the family name. Unfortunately Dobkin never quite grew out of the resemblance, so even though he's all of six now, he looks like a wise old man in little kid's clothes. Even Dobkin's day-care teachers always said he had an ancient soul. But on this particular morning he was even more perceptive than usual.

"Hmmm," he said, studying my face. "Better be careful."

There it was again . . . that warning. I glanced at Aunt Celia but she only nodded, waved, and hotrodded off down the street to drop Dobkin off at his own school three blocks away.

For a long time I just stood there on the sidewalk facing Edison High and wishing I was back in Florida. Not that I'd particularly enjoyed anything there except getting a good tan . . . but at least we'd lived there long enough for it to seem familiar. See, that's where Dobkin and I are different. It takes me a long time to adjust to a new place, but Dobkin fits right in wherever he happens to be. And Aunt Celia never stays in one place very long.

"With a whole wonderful world out there, we have no excuse ever to be bored!" is what she's always telling us—which is why we're always packing up the very second that school lets out and moving off somewhere else. She's got it down to a system, really. She calls a family conference, and then she takes out a map of the United States, and then one of us gets to close our eyes and point our finger anywhere on the map while she moves it around to keep us from cheating. It was Aunt Celia's turn when we ended up in Florida with a cottage right on the beach. The time before that, Dobkin picked North Carolina, and we rented a real log cabin up in the mountains. So when my finger landed on Missouri this time, I knew Dobkin was disappointed because lately he's been obsessing about Texas and owning a cattle ranch.

"Why Missouri?" he'd asked me, narrowing his eyes, like I'd done it on purpose just to ruin his life.

"I don't know," I told him. "My finger just wanted to go there."

"Yeah, right," Dobkin grumbled.

I couldn't really blame him for being grumpy—it couldn't have happened at a worse time. Weeks of rain in Florida had flooded the town, the school, *and* our house—so Aunt Celia had decided to make the move a little early and let us finish out the school year somewhere else.

"The Midwest is lovely!" Aunt Celia had tried to cheer Dobkin up. "A lovely place to be! We'll find one of those wonderful small towns where everyone knows everyone else, and life is simple and honest and sweet."

Aunt Celia is one of those positive-thinking kinds of people. She's scatterbrained and creative and totally unpredictable, which makes life an exciting place to be as long as you're with her. I also think she must be very rich, since she never seems to sell any of her sculpture but can still afford to take us so many places—she's never talked about money, and I've never asked. She's taken care of us ever since our parents died in a car crash two years ago, and she's the only mother I've got, so I think she's pretty great in spite of all her weirdness.

But now here I was, glancing longingly over my shoulder, watching the van grow smaller and smaller as it went down the street and left me behind. And then I swallowed the lump in my throat and turned back to the ugly building.

"Come on," I muttered to myself, squaring my shoulders and taking one step forward. It always makes me feel better when I talk out loud. "It's not like this is the first time you've ever had to do this."

Yet how was I to know, standing there on the sidewalk of Edison High School, that this time was going to be different?

"Come on," I said to myself again. "Get going."

And I was so determined to be brave that I swung my shoulder purse out to my side and then behind me in a big wide arc without even looking first.

I felt the impact only a second before I heard the gasp.

Spinning around, I was horrified to see a guy right behind me, doubled over and holding his stomach. His books were scattered across the sidewalk, and his black hair hung down all around his face so that I couldn't actually see what he looked like. I was so shocked, all I could do was stand there and stare. After what seemed like forever, he finally straightened up and stared back at me, and when I saw the corners of his mouth twitch, I wasn't sure if he was getting ready to yell or just trying not to laugh.

"I hope you have that thing registered," he said softly. He was wearing an overcoat way too big for him—a long flowing black thing buttoned right down over his black hightops. He was also wearing a black baseball cap, turned around backward.

"Wh-what?" I stammered.

"Lethal weapon." He kept a straight face. "What do you have inside that thing? Rocks?"

"I'm so sorry." Dropping my purse onto the sidewalk, I went toward him, but he jumped back out of reach.

"Whoa!" He shook his head. "I can't take any more pain today, thanks very much."

"I said I was sorry," I babbled. "I didn't hear you coming."

"I'm sneaky."

He threw me a curious glance, as though he wanted to know about me but was too polite to ask, and then he shifted his attention to his books spread out all over the sidewalk. With one quick movement he squatted down and started gathering up his things.

"Here—let me help," I offered, but he held out one hand to ward me off.

"No. That's okay. Stay where you are."

Now that he wasn't watching me, I could see how

really cute he was, how soft his hair looked as he shook it back from his wide dark eyes. He was slender and had sort of delicate features—small nose, narrow chin, and cheekbones and eyelashes I would have died for—and his body moved with this easy grace that was incredibly sexy. I wondered if he had any idea what kind of effect he must have on girls. He straightened back up and arched an eyebrow at me.

"I don't know you," he said. His smile was kind of teasing but also kind of shy, so I smiled back.

"I'm new. This is my first day."

He gave a slight nod. "And you live over on Walnut Street. And you just moved here."

"How do you know where I live?" I asked, surprised.

He didn't say anything, only smiled again. Flustered, I looked away and tried to sound nonchalant.

"Well, you're right, we did just move. From Florida."

"From Florida to *here?*" He looked from one end of the peaceful tree-lined street to the other. "Why?"

"My aunt's got a wandering spirit," I said, trying to make a joke. "And when the mood strikes her . . ."

I left the sentence unfinished. His eyes were almost as black as his hair—now that I could see them in the light—and very wide set in the slender lines of his face. It made him look kind of whimsical and innocent—yet I couldn't help noticing how he never quite focused in on me when he talked.

"Look," I said for the third time, "I'm really sorry about hitting you. I should have looked behind me."

He didn't say a word. He lifted his hand slowly to

my cheek and barely touched it with his fingertips. Startled, I felt shivers shoot straight down through my feet, rooting me to the sidewalk.

"I like your perfume," he said as his fingers slid away from my face. "Come on. I'll show you where the office is."

I felt like someone must feel when they've had a jolt of electricity go through them. My knees were so rubbery, I could hardly walk. I followed him up the steps and into the building, and thanked him as he dropped me off at the first door.

"It was right on my way." He seemed embarrassed by my gratitude. "Oh . . . I'm Tyler."

"Hi. Marlee Fleming."

"See you in class, Marlee Fleming."

He was walking backward, weaving through the flow of students hurrying off to their homerooms, yet somehow managing to avoid running into anyone. Waving, I started to turn away when suddenly he stopped and pointed a finger at me.

"You be careful," he said.

He was smiling.

But it was the third time I'd heard those words that morning.

And warnings always come in threes.

2

It happened before I even got to my first class.

I was hoping it wouldn't take long to register, since Aunt Celia had already talked with Mr. Hayden, the principal, the day before, but by the time I finally got my schedule, homeroom was over and the halls were swarming with kids. I could feel stares boring into me as I came out of the office, but before I could figure out which direction to go, there was a shout behind me and someone tugged on my sleeve.

"Hey, Marlee, wait up!"

The girl at my side was much shorter than I was, and very petite—tiny bones, tiny hands, tiny heart-shaped face—but her laugh carried clearly over the yelling in the corridor and relaxed me at once.

"Didn't you hear me calling?" she scolded and laughed again, a carefree giggle that made me want to laugh with her. "You forgot your locker assignment," she added, waving a piece of paper in front of my nose. "And of course, *me*—your official guide to show you around!"

Her grin was as contagious as her laugh. Her blue eyes crinkled up into little slits, and she ran one hand back through a short mop of frizzy brown hair.

"I'm Noreen Peterson." She grabbed my hand and pumped it up and down with surprising strength for such a little person. "Welcome to Edison. You *did* just move here—isn't that what I heard?"

I nodded. "Over the weekend. But we're not really settled yet."

"It takes a while," Noreen agreed. "But you're only renting, aren't you? So it's not like you have to worry about bringing a lot of stuff, 'cause the place already has furniture, right? If," she added thoughtfully, "you could call all that junk furniture."

She linked her arm through mine and bulldozed me through the packed throngs of students, totally oblivious to their rude remarks and teasing as she ran them down.

"How do you know so much about it?" I asked her, and she stopped again, leaning close with a giggle.

"That you're renting old lady Turley's place? 'Cause my mom's the realtor." She shrugged and gave me a pat on the shoulder. "But even if she weren't, I'd still know about it. *Everyone* knows when something happens here. You'll get used to that after a while."

"So who was old lady Turley?" I asked, trying to keep up with her again as she sped off down the hall.

"Edison's personal pain in the butt," Noreen replied, waiting for me to catch up. "Snooped on the neighbors, complained all the time, had a zillion cats. She hated kids. Always complained we ruined her yard taking shortcuts through it. She loved to yell horrible things at us . . . so of course that's why we kept cutting through her yard."

I thought of the little yellow house tucked back from its picket fence, and the huge old trees sagging comfortably over its roof, and the climbing roses on the front gate, and the lilac bushes blooming by the back steps. Mentally I went through each of its small old-fashioned rooms cluttered with outdated furniture and useless antiques, and I thought of the upstairs bedroom I'd chosen for myself, a corner one with sprigged wallpaper and windows on two walls, with views of the backyard and the empty weed-grown lot behind that and the quiet wooden houses that sat next door.

"It's not that bad, I guess," I finally spoke up. "It's just that the house seems so old, and the furniture is really depressing."

"Well," Noreen said philosophically, "Miss Turley was practically a hundred when she died, after all. How much taste could she have had?" She thought a minute, then added, "How come you wanted *that* house? You could have rented one of the apartments over on Cleveland Street—they're gorgeous."

I felt bad when I heard that. "Well . . . my aunt likes houses with character," I said lamely. "And she wanted to live in a real neighborhood for a change. Where she could get to know people."

"Imagine that." Noreen looked slightly awed. "I've lived here my whole life and never even thought about it. I've always had neighbors and known everyone in town." She shook her head and dragged me off again. "Maybe your aunt could renovate that old house— make it nice again? That would sure impress everyone!"

"Do we need to?" I couldn't help asking.

"Need to what?"

"Impress everyone."

Noreen giggled. "Just the fact that you moved to Edison at all is impressive! Everyone's wondering why!" She sighed and shook her head. "People are really nice here, but they probably won't accept you right away. So don't take it personally. That's just the way it is—nothing ever changes, no one ever leaves, and if you haven't done anything to make the neighbors gossip, they'll make something up!"

She swerved me sharply around a corner, pointing out various doorways as we rushed past.

"There's the library, if you want to call it that— there's the girls' bathroom, one of them, anyway—the newspaper office is that room to the left, and Miss Crane, our counselor—she's old and senile, you know, like what could she possibly know about kids— lurks over there behind that door. Okay—that room —that'll be your homeroom—Miss Arnett, same as mine—the door at the end of the hall leads outside, cafeteria to the right, gym to the left—"

She broke off and waited for me to say something, so I nodded to show her I was keeping up with the tour. As five kids shouted something from the other side of the corridor, Noreen pointed at my head and shouted back.

"The new girl! Her name's Marlee!"

I didn't have to worry about telling anyone hello. Noreen clutched my arm tighter and hustled me off again before I could open my mouth.

"How big was your last school?" she asked.

"Well . . ." I had to stop and think. "About five hundred in the senior class."

"Well, there're *two* hundred here, and that's with *all* the classes." She shook her head and made a face at me. "Before next period's over, everyone will know your name, where you're from, and all the dark secrets of your past. Don't let the stares bother you. I know you feel like you're on display, but the truth is, they're all jealous of you."

"Jealous of me?" I sounded shocked. "Why—"

"Because you're from somewhere else. And nobody here has ever been somewhere else. Come on, I want to show you some more stuff."

"But what about class?"

"Hey, this is part of the initiation process," she scolded me, "and I love being out of class, so I'm going to show you everything I can think of. Which should take all of . . . five minutes, if we're lucky."

The bell rang and everyone scattered. Noreen and I stood against the wall and watched kids stream out in every direction, funneling into open doorways until the hall lay empty and still around us.

"I'll take you upstairs. And then I'll show you the auditorium. And then we'll go to your locker, and then I'll take you to class, 'cause I'm going there, too."

13

She squeezed my arm and grinned an impish grin.

"Don't worry—in just a few days you'll be breezing around here like you grew up in Edison with the rest of us. And if you need anything at all—I mean *anything*—just let me know."

It's funny how some people just seem to click with the very first meeting. That's how I felt about Noreen, though I was trying really hard not to. Living with Aunt Celia, I've learned not to make friends too easily because I know I'll just end up leaving them. But Noreen made me *want* to be friends, no matter if I left again or not.

She was right about the school. It took about two more minutes to cover the rest of the classrooms, and then she hauled me out the back door and showed me the athletic field, then the gym, the cafeteria and snack bar, and finally the auditorium. The campus was small but much nicer than some I'd been to—there were trees everywhere and benches and even picnic tables for eating outside on nice days.

"Ahhh, if spring would just get here and *stay* here . . ." Noreen took a last longing glance over her shoulder as she ushered me back into the main building again, and I nodded.

"I'm not used to your cold weather," I said.

"It's not usually this chilly in spring—though it *has* been known to snow at Easter!" Noreen sighed. "Things are blooming and we're still stuck in jackets—I want sunshine and swimsuits!" She shut her eyes as if dreaming of summer, and let out a huge sigh. "Come on, let's go to your locker, and then we'll

14

brave Mrs. Clark's history class. If we're really lucky, she'll spend so much time making you feel at home, she'll forget about the test we're supposed to have today!"

I had to laugh. As Noreen raced off again, she glanced at the piece of paper in her hand and quickly scanned the rows of lockers we were passing. Finally she stopped at the end of the hall, and as I caught up with her, I saw her stare at the top locker, then down at the paper, then up at the locker again.

"Is there a problem?" I asked, coming up behind her. "If it's already taken, I'll just go back to the office and ask—"

"No!" She whirled around, and for just a split second her smile had this odd little twist to it, almost like someone had pasted it there on her face. But then it melted into her familiar grin again, and I knew I must have imagined it.

"I mean . . . no, it's not taken," she said. "This one wouldn't be taken. As you can see, it's perfectly empty."

I couldn't really see, because the door was closed, but I followed the point of her finger to the end locker on the top row.

"Here it is," Noreen said. "Right here. You can go ahead and put your jacket in if you want—the building's always hotter than anyone can stand."

I was watching her as she talked, but she wasn't looking at me now, and she wasn't looking at the locker, either. Her eyes were fixed on some vague spot in the air above my head, and she was shoving the piece of paper into my hand as if she didn't want to hold it anymore. After throwing her a puzzled glance, I read the combination, then reached up to open the door.

"That's funny." I frowned. "I can't get the lock open."

I tried the combination again, holding my breath as I twisted the dial. When I reached the last digit, I pulled at the latch, but it still wouldn't give.

"There must be a mistake," I told Noreen. "It must be the combination to some other locker."

"I don't think so," she said quietly.

"Here. Hold my purse, will you?"

Determined now, I took the lock in both hands, gritted my teeth, and turned the knob slowly and carefully.

"Third time's a charm," I mumbled, and to my surprise, the door popped open so suddenly that if I hadn't known better, I'd have sworn something heaved it out at me from inside. The impact sent me sprawling back several steps, right into Noreen, who put up her hands to steady me.

"Must have just been stuck," I said, relieved. "I hope it doesn't do that every time I need to get it op—"

I never got to finish my sentence.

As a sickening stench washed over me, I choked and started to gag, dimly aware of hands clutching my throat, clawing for air—

From far away someone called to me, but the hall was a total blur now—dark and brown and runny—

oozing down around me in a suffocating flood of darkness.

I opened my mouth and heard the screams.

But not my screams . . .

Screams of pain . . . horror . . . *agony* . . .

Screams coming from my locker.

3

Silence rushed in.

For an eternity I floated there in my strange, quiet darkness, every sense numb beyond feeling.

"Marlee . . . what's wrong . . ."

Reality slammed into me with a terrible jolt.

Lights overhead, rows of old lockers, peeling walls, scuffed floorboards—everything hit me at once, and I felt myself falling backward into a pair of arms that were all too real.

"Marlee! Marlee, are you *okay?"*

It was Noreen's voice, I recognized it now, but she was yelling, not whispering, and it wasn't her arms holding me up and literally keeping me from collapsing onto the floor.

"Are you all right?" Tyler demanded. His face was about two inches away from my own, and I could see

Noreen right behind him, peering anxiously around his shoulder.

"I . . ." My eyes grew wide as I looked at him. "What happened?"

"I thought you were going to faint!" Noreen's voice rose several octaves. "You looked so strange, and I saw Tyler coming out of class, and I yelled for him to help!"

"I'd be insulted," Tyler said in a stage whisper, "if someone told me *I* looked strange."

I gazed into his eyes and slowly put one hand to my forehead. Things were starting to focus now, crystal clear—*too* clear—so sharp and distinct that I wanted to block out each larger-than-life detail. I could see the little threads unraveling from one of Noreen's shoe-laces, and the tiny mole hidden behind her right ear; I could see the crooked finger on Tyler's left hand that might have been broken once, and the faded scar on his wrist beneath the cuff of his shirt.

"Should we get her to the nurse?" Noreen looked at Tyler, but I put my hand on her arm.

"No, I'm okay."

"You sure?"

"No," Tyler said, squinting at me. "I think she's going to cry."

"I'm not going to cry," I insisted, even though I'd never felt more like crying. "Just give me a minute."

"Can you stand up?" Noreen leaned over me, but when I didn't answer right away, she cupped her hands around her mouth. "I said, can you—"

"Hey, Noreen, why don't you talk a little louder so

everyone in the building will come out here to see what's wrong?" Tyler's look was mildly reproachful, but Noreen didn't seem to notice.

"Really," I said shakily, "I'm fine."

"Let's get her outside," Tyler said. "In the fresh air."

The next thing I knew, they were both guiding me out the door, and I was shaking so bad that I stumbled and fell right against Tyler's chest.

"Here you go, sit here," Tyler said. He lowered me carefully onto one of the concrete steps, and then he stood back and began to whistle softly, as if this sort of thing happened all the time and music always made it better.

"I'm so embarrassed," I mumbled. *No—it didn't really happen!* "I can't believe I did this." *No—I won't let it happen!* And I put my hands to my temples and pressed hard—harder—*no, no, it's not supposed to happen, I promised myself it would never happen again—*

"Marlee?" Noreen sat down beside me, and I felt her arm slip gently around my shoulders. And then suddenly things began to settle again . . . normally . . . everything in its right place and proper perspective. I looked up at Tyler, and he stopped whistling.

"It's okay," Noreen reassured me, giving me a hug, but her voice was quivering and her hands felt cold. "It's hard being the new kid in a new school, everyone staring at you, not knowing what to expect. It's really okay. Isn't it okay, Tyler?"

"It might be okay," Tyler said agreeably, "if you'd shut up for ten whole seconds."

He met Noreen's frown with a look of wide-eyed innocence, but there was this little twinkle way back behind his stare. I couldn't tell if he was amused at my stupid predicament or at Noreen's overreaction—she seemed almost as upset as I was. My hands were still trembling, and I clasped them together so he and Noreen wouldn't notice. *It wasn't supposed to come back—wasn't supposed to happen—how could it—how could it—*

"I told you to be careful," Tyler reminded me, a slow smile easing across his lips. "I bet you didn't even eat breakfast this morning, did you?"

"This doesn't have anything to do with eating." I didn't mean to sound so defensive, but I was scared and queasy and still trying to shut down all the confusion in my brain. "It was the smell in that locker."

Tyler looked at Noreen and Noreen looked at me, and I looked back at the door as if the smell might come pouring out on top of me at any second.

"I've never smelled anything like that before. What do you think it was?"

Even now the horrible odor still lingered in my mind. Pressing one hand to my throat, I fought off a wave of nausea and suddenly realized that Tyler and Noreen were staring at me, not saying a word. I felt my cheeks grow hot, and I fanned myself with one hand and tried to laugh.

"Well. I guess whoever had that locker before me forgot to fumigate it."

What's wrong with them—why aren't they smiling?

It was a joke! Why aren't they saying anything—why are they staring at me like that—

"What smell?" Noreen finally asked in a small voice.

This time it was my turn to stare. "You're not serious, are you? You couldn't have been standing that close to me and not smelled it. It practically knocked me over!"

Noreen's brows knitted together and she chewed her lip.

"I . . ." She glanced quickly at Tyler. "Maybe I just didn't notice—"

"You couldn't *not* have noticed." I looked her full in the face, dumbfounded by her answer. "You must have—you *had* to—"

I broke off as Tyler took my elbows and hauled me to my feet. He held the door open for Noreen and me, and then he sauntered back down the hallway. Pausing in front of the open locker, he leaned slowly forward till his head was inside. Then he turned around and faced us with a look of mock horror.

"The gym socks that wouldn't die!"

"Come on, Tyler," Noreen mumbled, "can't you see she's serious?"

His smile faded. "Okay, sorry. There's no smell."

"It can't be gone—that's just impossible." Pushing past Tyler, I stuck my own head inside the locker, but after a few seconds, I pulled back out again, bewildered.

"But it *was* here," I insisted. "I mean . . . it was so strong!"

Noreen took a cautious sniff, hesitated, then took a second one for good measure.

"I don't smell anything," she said weakly, and again I caught the quick look she shot at Tyler.

"What exactly did it smell like?" Tyler asked me.

I stared from one of them to the other. I knew my mouth was hanging open, so I closed it and swallowed hard and concentrated on looking halfway rational.

"It was so . . ."

I frowned. Only minutes ago every one of my senses had been brutally assaulted, but now I could barely remember what any of those feelings had been. *That's it . . . that's right . . . empty your mind . . . you can do it . . . just like you did the last time . . . just like you did when it hurt so bad . . .*

I shook my head slowly, trying to clear it. "I don't know *what* it smelled like, exactly. Horrible. Sickening. But I'm sure I'd know it if I ever smelled it again."

"Biology lab is right over there." Tyler gave a casual wave of his hand. "Probably some experiment going on. Something being dissected. You could have gotten a whiff of that."

"My friend Becky walked past the lab one time and keeled right over," Noreen said helpfully. "She was carrying a fishbowl to one of the other science rooms, and she fell on top of it and cut herself in eight places."

"Poor fish," Tyler said, and the corners of his mouth twitched as Noreen turned on him.

"Well, you know, Tyler, it really wasn't funny!" She sounded upset. "I know Becky is sort of . . . well . . .

heavy . . . but she didn't squash those fish on purpose!"

Tyler was trying so hard to look sympathetic and failing so miserably that I finally had to smile.

"It must have been the lab then," I lied, because I knew no stench like that could possibly have been there one minute, then faded so completely the next. I didn't want to talk about it anymore—didn't even want to think about it. I just wanted to go to class and lose myself in some boring lecture and forget about what had happened.

"Right, then, let's go," Noreen said quickly. She seemed as relieved as I was to drop the subject, and as she leaned over to brush off my skirt, Tyler stood watching her with a tolerant smile.

"I don't know what to say," I told him. "Seems like all I'm doing today is apologizing to you."

His smile widened in a lazy sort of way. "Are you always this much trouble to have around?"

"Maybe they're working on gas lines somewhere, and there's a leak," Noreen fretted. "That could really happen, couldn't it?"

Tyler gave a solemn nod. "Anything could happen, Noreen. I could get bitten by a werewolf tonight and spend the rest of my life running naked through the woods trying to find a good vet."

"Oh, please," Noreen said dryly, "the very image of you without your clothes is enough to give anyone severe nightmares."

She winced as Tyler shoved her from behind and sauntered away down the hall. He paused at the corner and saluted us before he disappeared, and Noreen turned to me with a sigh.

"I'm only kidding, you understand."

"About what?" I asked.

"About Tyler. Actually, he doesn't look half bad without his clothes. Actually"—she sighed again—"he looks pretty damn wonderful."

I glanced down at my watch. "Shouldn't we get to class?"

"He's very modest," Noreen went on, leaning in close to my ear. "Kind of shy, really. How was I supposed to know a bunch of the guys were skinny-dipping when I drove out to his cabin that day? He should have told me not to come. Was that my fault?"

I was only half listening. Noreen was talking really fast, carrying on this one-sided conversation and walking out into the hall again, but my locker was still open, and I couldn't stop staring at it. Just a locker, I told myself sternly. One that looks like all the others around it. *Nothing unusual about an old empty locker* . . .

But I was still shaky. I made myself go over and close the door, and then I told myself I must have imagined the whole thing, and I wasn't going to think about it anymore.

"Thank you," I said, and Noreen broke off chattering to look at me in surprise.

"For what?" She smiled.

"For not laughing," I said. "For not thinking I'm crazy."

"Hey, come on—"

"For trying to come up with some excuse so it won't get around the whole school that I'm some kind of disaster."

She looked at me sympathetically. "You're not a disaster. Now, Tyler . . . that's disaster." She waited for me to laugh, but when I didn't, she added cautiously, "What do you—*really*—think happened when you opened your locker?"

I frowned, trying to recall exact details, yet I knew I'd already buried them in some forbidden memory zone.

"Something happened," I said simply. "Whatever I smelled was coming from"—I stopped myself and proceeded cautiously—"*seemed* to be coming from that locker. Like whoever used it before me had something really disgusting stored in there and—"

"That's impossible." Noreen shook her head. "It hasn't been used for . . ." She hesitated and seemed to be searching for words. "For a long time," she finished at last. "Not since last fall, anyway."

"What do you mean? How do you know that?"

Her face looked so serious now, it was making me nervous. I waited for her to answer, and she finally said, "Because I knew the girl who had it last."

For a long time she didn't say anything else. We both stood there in the hall, and I could hear muffled classroom noises up and down the passageway and the faint faraway slam of a door, and then Noreen put her hand on my arm.

"It was Suellen's locker," she murmured. "Suellen Downing."

Just the way she said the name made me feel weird.

When I didn't respond, Noreen glanced up at me and then away again, as if she really didn't want to talk about it anymore.

"Who's that?" I heard myself ask, even though every instinct was telling me not to.

"A girl who went to school here," Noreen said softly. "Before she disappeared."

4

Disappeared?" I saw Noreen take a step forward, but I just kept standing there in the middle of the hall looking at her. "What do you mean, disappeared?"

"I mean she just vanished into thin air." Noreen gave a little shiver, then took my elbow and steered me down the hall, keeping her voice low. "You're bound to hear about it sooner or later—it's our town's one claim to fame. Or is it infamy?" She gave a wry smile. "One day she was here, and I was walking with her just like I'm walking with you now, and we were laughing and everything was normal. And then . . ."

She stopped walking. Her voice lowered even more, and her fingers tightened on my arm.

"No one knows what happened to her after school that day. No one ever saw her again . . . or heard from her."

I could feel myself nodding as I gazed into Noreen's eyes. For a moment I thought they filled with tears, but she blinked quickly and gave me a thin smile.

"That must have been so horrible," I murmured.

"For everyone. You never think something like that's going to happen to someone you know. Only this time it did."

Her words made me feel cold inside. I leaned back against the wall, but then Noreen was pulling on me again, and I had to go with her.

"Come on. I'd better get you to class before you fall down. Tyler has gym this period, so he won't be around to help me pick you up."

She grinned, and I was glad we were changing the subject. As she stopped outside the closed door of a classroom and hurriedly flipped through one of her notebooks, there was just one more question I had to ask.

"Tyler . . ." I said as casually as I could. "Is he your boyfriend?" Part of me was dying to know, while another part was bracing to be disappointed. When Noreen didn't answer, I thought she hadn't heard me, but then she looked up and moaned and slammed her notebook shut.

"I'm going to kill that Tyler—he forgot to give my notes back, and I need them for this class!" She cast me a long-suffering look and then giggled. "Me and Tyler? Are you kidding? We've been buddies since kindergarten—that's bad enough."

"Wow. That long?" Again I tried to sound nonchalant, but she was looking at me with a knowing twinkle in her eyes. "He seems nice," I added lamely.

She put her hand on the doorknob and looked back at me with that impish smile.

"Yeah," she said, her own voice just as casual. "He is."

I was glad to go into class then. I had this feeling that for all my efforts, I hadn't fooled Noreen for a second.

The day went by in a blur, and I was just as miserable as I always was in a new school, only this time it was worse. It wasn't that everyone wasn't nice to me—because they were—but I could still feel their stares and hear their whispers and I hated that feeling of being on display.

Except it wasn't just that.

No matter how hard I tried to concentrate, I couldn't stop thinking about what had happened that morning at my locker, and each time I remembered, I felt sick all over again. It just didn't make any sense—especially with the locker being empty all those months—yet I knew I hadn't imagined that smell. And the poor girl who'd used it before me, just disappearing off the face of the earth . . .

The whole thing gave me the creeps. If it hadn't been for Noreen, I don't know how I would have made it through that first day. Each time the bell rang, she magically appeared to whisk me off to my next class or lunch or gym or more classes again, and by the time school was over, I was in the hall looking for her, embarrassed that I'd come to depend so much on seeing her cheery face in the crowds.

"You survived!" she greeted me, grabbing my arm

and herding me down the corridor. "Congratulations!"

"Thanks to you," I said. "Your services went above and beyond."

"Oh, come on, I was glad to help." She brushed off my gratitude with a modest shake of her head. "But look at that load of books you're still carrying around —each time I see you, it's grown! How come you didn't dump all that stuff between classes?"

For a split second I wanted to tell her the truth, that I'd rather lug around everything I owned in the world than to go back to that locker again, but I realized how stupid that would sound. So instead I took a deep breath and lied.

"I thought I might have a spare minute in class to look things over. You know, to see if I'd already had some of this stuff in my other school."

"You probably have." Noreen chuckled. "I mean, look around—not exactly what you'd call progressive, right? Hey, a bunch of us are getting together later, and I thought it might be a good chance for you to meet some more of the kids. How about it?"

I shook my head. "That's really nice of you. But I have to stop by for my brother, and then my aunt's picking us up, and I promised I'd help her out at home."

"Where's your brother?" Noreen asked. "And is he cute?"

This time I laughed out loud. "Dobkin? He's at kindergarten and he's six years old. But you really should meet him sometime—if nothing else, he's pure entertainment."

Noreen waved as a small group shouted her name from the end of the hall.

"Coming! Look, Marlee." She turned back to me with a smile and touched me lightly on the shoulder. "I've got to run. Sure you won't change your mind? Sooner or later you'll have to face them all in person."

She laughed and I joined in, but I could feel a knot forming in the pit of my stomach.

"I will sometime," I hedged. "It's just that with moving in and all, the place is such a wreck and I promised my aunt—"

"See you!"

Before I could even finish, Noreen waved and hurried off, and I headed back in the opposite direction.

I was glad there were still a few kids hanging around in the hall. With them laughing and talking, it wasn't like anyone was really paying attention to me while I tried my locker combination. I don't even know what I expected, exactly—some horrible repeat of what had happened earlier, I guess—but instead the lock popped open easily in my hand, and the door swung out with no problem, and I just stood there staring into the empty little compartment.

And that's all it is . . . just an empty compartment. Nothing to be afraid of . . .

Shivering a little, I started to remember the incident all over again, so I shut my mind against it. Then I counted off homework assignments on my fingers and threw in the books I wouldn't be needing that night and slammed the door shut. In fact, I was trying so hard to get out of there that I didn't even notice the guy standing next to me, rummaging quietly through his own locker.

"So," a voice drawled. "You must be Marlee."

Startled, I glanced over, but the guy's face was hidden behind his open door. What I *could* see were tight jeans and narrow hips, dirty boots, and part of a denim sleeve. I started to say something, but he swung the door shut and beat me to it.

"Marlee Fleming," he said. "From Florida. You're renting the old Turley place."

It was said matter-of-factly and without any emotion. He hesitated a minute, then added, "Why Edison?"

He was so tall, I could feel my head bending backward just trying to look up into his face. Six feet four, I figured, with broad shoulders, and the rest of him sort of tapering down gradually into slim hard muscle. His hair was brushed straight back over his ears, touching his collar in back, and I could see all these different shades of blond in it—cornsilk and straw-gold and almost white on top. His face was rugged and deeply tanned—not the kind of tan you get in the summer, but more like he'd spent his whole life outdoors.

"Excuse me?" I managed to stammer.

"Why Edison?" he repeated, raking me with his eyes. They were an odd color—a mix of deep blue and deep green—and as they moved over me, they were so intense that I had to look away.

"Why *not* Edison?" I countered, keeping my gaze on my armload of books, pretending to sort through them one more time.

"No one would ever be transferred here, and I know for a fact you're not related to anyone in town." He paused, waiting for me to answer, but I didn't. "There must be some reason," he finally said.

"I don't have to have any reason," I replied. "It's a free country."

"Oh, I get it. Looking for a quaint little slice of Americana? Come to study the country bumpkins?"

He had this slow way of talking that made him sound lazy—almost indifferent—yet I could sense something just below the surface of his words—a sort of watchfulness, or wariness, that put me on my guard.

"I'm not that kind of person," I said stiffly. For a long moment his eyes stared full into mine, holding me so I couldn't look away. And then, to my surprise, he shook his head and turned his back on me.

"Well," he said softly, "we'll see."

I had no idea who he was, and as I hurried out of the building, I grew madder and madder. I felt like I'd been deliberately baited—put to some test or something—and I didn't like it one bit.

Dobkin's school was just minutes away, and it made me feel good to see all the little kids laughing and playing inside the fenced yard. I wasn't surprised to see my brother off by himself in a corner by the sandbox, flipping through a picture book and looking totally bored with his surroundings. One of the teachers asked me the password then started waving to Dobkin, telling him it was time to go home.

"So how was school?" I greeted him as he came strolling out. His little backpack was hanging lopsided over one shoulder, and his chubby hands were stained as purple as his sweatshirt.

"Oh, you know"—he sighed—"they're all such children."

I hid a smile and nodded as we started down the sidewalk. "What's with the new skin tone?"

"Dye," he said.

Again I nodded. You can't rush Dobkin. You have to let him take his time and tell things his own way, or he'll just clam up and not talk at all.

"One of the kids really liked my shirt. He said he'd trade me his shirt for mine 'cause he really liked purple."

This time I cringed.

"Of course I didn't want his shirt," Dobkin went on indignantly. "You never know where another kid's shirt has been."

He looked at me for confirmation, and I made a sympathetic sound in my throat.

"So I told him I'd dye his shirt to look like mine."

I pressed my lips tight. I could feel a laugh coming, but I managed to keep a straight face.

"So," Dobkin said solemnly, "when they passed out the grape juice—"

"I get the picture," I said.

"The kid loved it," Dobkin added.

"But the teacher didn't, I bet."

He cast me a sidelong glance and shook his head.

"Teachers have no sense of humor."

"No," I agreed, and he sighed.

"So what about you?" he asked. "What happened?"

"What do you mean, what happened?"

"I told you to be careful, but something probably happened anyway," he said matter-of-factly. "So what happened?"

I stopped on the sidewalk. A few steps ahead of me Dobkin stopped, too, although he didn't turn around.

"My locker attacked me," I said.

"That'd make such a great movie."

"I mean it, Dobkin. Something . . . *something's* wrong somewhere that I don't understand."

"But I probably will," he said. "So tell me."

I did.

I told him exactly how it had happened—exactly what I'd felt—senses sharpened, panic heightened— and the way I'd gone queasy and faint, and that sickening, disgusting odor. And when I'd finished, I realized I'd begun to tremble again, and that Dobkin had finally turned around and was staring at me with his wise funny face.

"You know what it is," he said solemnly.

"What?"

"The smell," he said. "You know what it is."

"No." I shook my head at him, and as I kept repeating "No—no—" I could feel my head shaking faster and my hands quaking harder, and I could see Dobkin nodding at me, up and down, up and down, not changing his grim expression.

"Yes, you do," he said, "so quit blocking it out of your mind."

"I *don't* know," only now I was pleading with him, and I could feel myself crumbling inside, dark images, dark memories flying out of long forgotten corners in my mind. "That horrible smell—I couldn't stand it—the stench—"

"Fear," Dobkin murmured, and I broke off abruptly.

"What . . . what did you say?"

"The smell of fear." Dobkin's eyes gazed back at me, huge brown saucers filled with sadness. "You remember. You smelled it once before."

5

You shouldn't have brought that up!" I could hear my voice as from a long way off, and I was screaming at him, something I never do to Dobkin. "You promised you wouldn't! You *promised!*"

Dobkin looked so guilty. His head bent forward a little, and his mouth was pressed together into such a tight line that both his cheeks puffed out and I could see his double chin.

"You promised," I said again, only this time I started off down the sidewalk and didn't even hear the horn honking behind me as Aunt Celia drove up. I stopped in my tracks and turned to see Dobkin standing there, torn between running after me and jumping into the van. So I wheeled around and climbed inside, and he climbed into the front next to Aunt Celia, and neither of us spoke to each other all the way home. I know Aunt Celia noticed, but she was too tactful to say anything. Instead she just directed questions at each of us about how our days had gone, and didn't try to make us chitchat. Once we reached the house, I headed straight for my room while Dobkin hung around in the garage, pretending he'd lost something under one of the car seats.

I closed my door and locked it and threw myself down on the bed. And then I shut my eyes and tried to blank out Dobkin's accusation, but it kept echoing over and over in my head till I thought I'd scream.

"You remember . . . you smelled it once before. . . ."

"It's a coincidence," I muttered fiercely to myself. "It's a coincidence, that's *all* it is. It doesn't have anything to do with anything. The stupid door on the stupid locker was just stuck, and I shouldn't have gone to school on an empty stomach—"

Tears filled my eyes, and I buried my face in my pillow, trying not to remember but not being able to help it. That night two years ago . . . lying across my bed and trying to study for a test . . . that sick feeling in my stomach, making me weak, making me nauseated . . . and that awful stench—every nerve, every sense, every heartbeat screaming, on fire, twisting with pain and premonition . . .

"Dobkin," I whispered.

I'd gone into Dobkin's room that night. Sick and terrified, I'd gone straight into Dobkin's room, and I'd held him, and then the doorbell had rung.

I could still remember the sound of that doorbell. Shrieking and shrieking through our house that would never be the same again.

"I'm afraid there's been an accident. . . ."

And I'd held Dobkin all through the night and then later all through the funeral, wondering what would happen to us now that both our parents were dead. . . .

"You remember . . . you smelled it once before. . . ."

"Oh, God."

The sound of my voice got through to me somehow. I raised my face from the bed and stared at my door, and then I got up and went across the room and opened it, knowing Dobkin would be standing there silently in the hall.

He was.

We looked at each other without saying a word, and he came in and perched on the foot of my bed while I locked the door behind him.

"Does Aunt Celia know?" I murmured at last.

"She knows you're upset, but I didn't tell her why," Dobkin said. "Maybe she thinks it's just nerves."

"Maybe that's all it is."

He gave me his most Dobkinish look, and I withered beneath it.

"Okay," I gave in. "So what *does* it mean?"

"The girl." He screwed up his face, deep in thought. "The one who disappeared. What do you know about her?"

"Just her name. Suellen something."

"She'd probably be easy to find out about. There must be newspaper articles."

"Come on." I sighed, flopping down on my back beside him, folding my arms beneath my head. "You realize we're getting into weird things here. You realize—"

"That is *not* what I'd call a normal locker," Dobkin reminded me sternly. "Maybe you stirred up something that's been wanting to get out."

"And somehow . . . I connected with it?" I mulled this over for several seconds. "A feeling of fear—no, that's not right—*terror*—from an old locker in an old school—most likely because I was so *nervous* about being there." I cast him a reluctant glance. "Okay, so let's say you *might* be on to something. *Might* be," I added grudgingly. "Whose terror did I connect with? Suellen's? Or just mine?"

He furrowed his brow, and his double chin tripled. "Both, maybe."

"Quit going psychic on me, Dobkin."

"You're the one who's psychic. I'm just trying to make you think. Listen. What did those other kids do when you almost passed out?"

"Noreen and Tyler? They kept me from falling on the floor! They stood there and watched me make a total fool of myself!"

"I mean"—Dobkin sighed loudly—"did they say something like, 'Oh, no, not that haunted locker again!'?"

"Haunted locker?" I propped myself on my elbows and gave him a scathing look. "That's the best one yet, Dobkin. As if I didn't have enough on my mind right now without—"

"You knew when Mom and Dad were killed. You knew the exact second it happened, even though we were miles and miles away. You can't deny that."

"Stop it," I muttered, turning over so he couldn't

see my face. "How would you remember, anyway? You were too little."

"I remember," he said softly.

We both went quiet then. I could hear Aunt Celia in the kitchen below us banging pots and pans and chopping something for dinner, and outside my window a tree branch scraped gently against the glass.

"If it happens again, you won't be able to ignore it," Dobkin challenged me. "If it happens again, you'll have to admit you've picked up on something. If it happens again—"

"It won't," I cut him off and swung my feet over the side of the bed. "Do you mind? I've got homework to do."

I hated ending it like that. I glanced over my shoulder and watched him trudge across the floor. He paused with one hand on the doorknob.

"If it happens again," Dobkin said reasonably, "what if something happens to *you?*"

I felt a chill go through me, deep and piercing. Somehow I managed to laugh.

"You're so silly, Dobkin. I thought Aunt Celia told you not to watch all those scary shows on TV anymore."

"The reason I watch them"—Dobkin gazed back over his shoulder at me—"is to keep alert to every possibility."

Dad's favorite expression . . . how did Dobkin remember that?

My heart clenched a little, remembering the wink Dad always used to give me when he doled out advice, and I just looked at Dobkin, not really sure what to say. He shut the door behind him, and I wandered over to my back window and stared out.

At one time the backyard must have been beautiful, with all its trees and shrubs and even what looked like a small plot of garden in one corner beside the storage shed. Someone had been nice enough to mow the grass before we moved in, but weeds still marched along the fence and choked the flowerbeds where a few sorry tulips had managed to stick their heads through. A dream for Aunt Celia, I thought—she'd be spending hours and hours out there trying to turn the place into some sort of exotic paradise.

I let my gaze roam slowly to the neighbor's backyard on the right. I could see only part of it—a doghouse and some apple trees—but there was no sign of movement anywhere. It made me realize suddenly that no one had come over to welcome us since we'd been here—but then again, we'd only shown up late Friday night, and the weekend had been taken up with trying to settle in and run errands and stock up the refrigerator. *Still . . . you'd think in a small town where everyone's supposed to be so curious about you . . .*

Restlessly I moved to the other windowpane, turning my attention to the neighbor's house on the left. One second-story window was practically opposite my own, yet it was hard to really see because of the huge old oak tree in our side yard. Its trunk was at least ten feet around, and its massive branches spread out so far, I could easily have crawled out and perched on them. There were more thick heavy limbs stretching all the way across the fence to that upstairs window, making a kind of bridge between the houses. Sliding open the sash, I let the cool air blow across my cheeks as I stared out into the lengthening shadows of late afternoon. We were supposed to have screens put on the windows, but they'd had to be special ordered and hadn't come in yet, so I could hang out as far as I wanted. Squinting, I tried to see if anyone was visible in that window next door. For one second I thought I saw curtains moving, but I couldn't be sure.

"If it happens again, what if something happens to you?"

I tried not to think about what Dobkin had said, but I couldn't help it. He has such a wild imagination, and he always tries to sound so mysterious when he's offering words of wisdom—but this time it really got to me.

Come on, Marlee, give it a rest. I mean, look around! What could be more peaceful than this boring place?

Peaceful . . .

A little town where nothing ever happens.

And when Aunt Celia decided it was time to move again, I closed my eyes and moved my hand back and forth over the map, and watched my finger land right on this spot, just as surely as if some invisible force had grabbed it and slammed it smack down on top of Edison.

"That's not true," I mumbled. "It *seemed* that way, but I could have picked anywhere. Anywhere at all."

Shivering, I closed my eyes and just stood there, feeling the breeze on my cheeks, listening to it sift through the oak leaves and sigh around the eaves of the house.

And then . . . slowly . . . my skin began to prickle.

Eyes wide now, I drew back into my room, hands clenched tightly on the sill.

Someone's watching me.

I knew it just as surely as I was standing there, could *feel* it, hidden and silent and cold—*so very cold*—*eyes without emotion*—*without feeling*—*empty* . . .

"Aunt Celia," I whispered, but of course she didn't hear.

No one heard as I stood there, too terrified to move—trapped by something I couldn't even see—

"Aunt Celia!" I screamed.

From faraway I heard a muffled voice and then footsteps running up the stairs.

But I didn't need Aunt Celia now.

I knew that whoever had been watching me was gone.

6

What on earth's the matter!"

I can only imagine what I must have looked like, standing there with my back pressed against the wall, arms out to my sides, trying to breathe normally again. Poor Aunt Celia rushed over to me and put an arm around my shoulders and led me straight over to the bed.

"You're as white as a ghost! What happened?"

"I thought I felt something," I mumbled. "I mean, I *did* feel something . . . I don't know . . ."

"What, dearest? What did you feel?"

"Eyes." My voice dropped and I leaned against her, still trembling. "I felt eyes watching me——"

"Eyes!"

"But I don't feel them now." Gently I disentangled myself from her arms and ran one hand across my forehead. "Really. I'm okay."

"I told you," Dobkin said.

I hadn't noticed him standing in the doorway, and now he came into my room, exchanging solemn looks with Aunt Celia. I wished they'd go away and quit fussing—I felt silly now for making such a commotion, and I hated the way both of them had stopped looking at each other and were now staring straight at me.

"I'm just tired," I insisted crossly. "You know how hard it is for me when I start a new school."

"Hmmm." Aunt Celia redirected her gaze onto the floor, and her lips pressed into a thin line—a sure sign she was thinking really hard before she said something. At last she added, "You looked so strange this morning."

"I look like I always do!" My voice rose defensively. "If that means I look strange, I can't help it if that's the way I look."

I knew I was sounding childish, but I couldn't seem to stop myself.

"Maybe we should have a discussion," Aunt Celia began helpfully, but I jumped off the bed and pushed past Dobkin out into the hallway.

"I'm going to take a walk," I announced.

Aunt Celia jumped up after me and nodded with forced brightness. "What a great idea! Fresh air will do you good."

"Coward," Dobkin mumbled, but I ignored him and ran down the stairs and out the front door.

For several minutes I just stood there on the porch, waiting for my heart to settle down into my chest again. I could smell early flowers and the hint of rain in the air, and the freshness of new leaves just out on the trees. I leaned for a while on the porch rail, but then, as I straightened up again and glanced at the house next door, I realized someone was sitting over there in the porch swing.

"Hi," said the voice, and I caught my breath in surprise.

"Tyler?" I asked cautiously.

"Yeah."

He sprang into full view and draped his body lazily over the front railing. I could see he wasn't wearing his coat now—just jeans and a black sweatshirt with holes in it—but the cap was still turned around on his head and his hightops had come unlaced. As I watched, he pulled off the cap, shook his hair out of his eyes, then smashed the cap down onto his head again, lopsided.

"Hi," he said again quietly. "You look surprised."

"Shouldn't I be?" My tone was accusing. "What are you doing?"

"I live here."

"You do?" I must have sounded shocked, because there was the slightest touch of laughter in his voice.

"Yeah. I do."

"Why didn't you tell me?"

"Why didn't you ask?"

"Well, I usually don't go into a new school asking every kid I meet, hey, do you live next door to me?" I was sort of embarrassed, like he'd played a trick on me. "I didn't see you around this weekend."

"I wasn't here," he said, not offering to tell me where he'd been. "I just got back late last night."

"Oh." I didn't know what else to say. Tyler hopped lightly up onto the railing, his arms straight out at his sides, as if walking a tightrope.

"You as crazy as old lady Turley?" he asked casually.

"I might be," I said.

"Just wondering." Again that hint of laughter in his voice, though he kept his face expressionless. I watched him and thought how jealous I was again of his perfect skin and those perfect eyelashes and that perfectly formed mouth.

"You're thinking . . . you've seen me in some other lifetime," he said, and I snapped back to awareness.

"I'm not thinking anything about you," I lied.

"That's why you keep looking at my face. Am I familiar to you? Did we meet in some other dimension? Were we friends or maybe lovers?"

"I wasn't looking at your face."

"Yes, you were." He hopped off the railing and landed at the very bottom of the porch steps. He slid his hands into the pockets of his jeans and leaned lazily against one wooden column of the porch.

"So how's it feel living in the museum?"

I almost laughed at that. "Like a museum."

"Maybe you should sell tickets and take tours through."

"Maybe. I could use the spending money."

"So how was your first day? Any more confrontations with your locker?"

"I don't want to talk about that."

"How come?"

"It was very upsetting. And embarrassing. And you'll just laugh."

"No, I won't."

This time he crossed his yard, leapt lightly over the fence, then stood there staring up at me as I watched from my porch.

"That was Suellen Downing's locker," he said.

"I heard. A girl who disappeared."

He nodded. His brown eyes looked almost sad.

"She was a nice girl. I liked her."

"Did you grow up with her, too?"

"No." Squatting down, he ran his long fingers slowly over the ivy that grew up through the cracks in the walkway. "She was an outsider. Her dad was on the construction crew that came through Edison when the new highway was being built. She and her family were only living here till his job was over."

I let this sink in, feeling a prickle race up my spine. "Did her family happen to rent *this* house?"

He looked surprised. "No. They had a place outside of town. Why?

Now I felt stupid. "No reason. I was just curious."

"So is it?" he asked me.

"Is what what?"

"Your house like a museum?"

I had to laugh. "You can come in if you want. Check for dead teenagers in the basement."

He looked at me, and his smile seemed sort of strained, and for just a split second everything seemed to freeze around him, as if I were looking at a movie still.

"No, thanks," he said casually. "Some things are better left un—" But before he could say anything else, a woman came outside and called to him, something about not forgetting what he was supposed to do before dinner.

"I have to go." He jumped up and swung himself back over the fence into his own yard. "See you around."

"Yeah," I said. "See you."

He started toward his house, then stopped in his tracks and spun around to face me.

"Why don't you come?" he asked.

"Me?" I looked around wildly, as if there might be four or five other people standing around behind me that he might be talking to.

"Yeah. Come with me. I'm just going out to Lost River. I won't be long."

"I . . . uh . . . have homework to do."

"Do it later."

"Well . . ."

"Do it later. I'll help you."

I shook my head at the offer, but as I stared into those big dark eyes, my heart betrayed me. What girl could have resisted an offer like that?

"I'll have to tell my aunt," I said.

"Go do it."

It only took a second to make my announcement and grab my jacket, and then I was back out again, hurrying to meet him where he now waited in his driveway next to a battered old gray Mustang.

"Okay?" Tyler let the hood crash down. He wiped

his hands on a rag, wadded it up, and tossed it onto the porch. Then he tilted his head at me with a sidelong glance.

"Hope you like bumpy rides."

"I don't mind them," I said.

"Good. Climb in."

I did, and he did, and then without warning, the car gave a tremendous lurch and bounced off, throwing me right up against him as I desperately tried to keep my balance.

"Sorry!" I shouted. The windows were wide open, and I could hardly hear myself think, and as I struggled to hold on to the door handle, the car swerved and I bounced right into him again. "Sorry!" I yelled for the second time, but he only gave me that faint little smile and made the Mustang go faster.

It didn't take long to get out into the country.

Since the ride was too bumpy and noisy for conversation, I concentrated on the scenery as we sped along, noticing how we turned off the main highway and then, after several miles down a two-lane blacktop, off again onto a dirt road. It got quieter then, and we slowed down nearly to a crawl, winding back and back through deep twisted woods. I wondered how anyone could ever find his way through there, with the shadows so deep and deceptive, and the early twilight almost full dark. I must have shivered a little because Tyler suddenly reached over and touched my arm.

"Cold?" he asked.

"Not really. It's just so dark out here."

He nodded, curling his body back into his seat,

resting one arm lazily across the top of the steering wheel.

"Country dark's not like any other kind of dark. And the river's even worse."

We rounded a bend in the road, and the headlights picked up a dilapidated little house far back from the curve. Obviously abandoned, it leaned a little to one side, and the weeds grew up as high as the shuttered windows.

"Suellen used to live there," Tyler said. "You know . . . the girl whose locker you have."

I moved closer to get a better view. Shadows angled down over the roof, spilling in black puddles across the sagging front porch.

I shuddered. "It looks haunted."

Tyler shrugged and began to whistle. His glance flicked briefly to me and then out his window again.

"Tell me about Suellen Downing," I said quietly.

He didn't act surprised at the request. In fact, he didn't act any way at all. He stared straight out at the curving road and thought for several moments and then smiled.

"She was nice," he finally said. "I didn't mind her."

"But what was she *like?* I mean . . . what kind of person was she?"

His eyebrow lifted, and his face took on a puzzled look. "Why all this interest in someone you don't even know?" When I didn't answer, he added softly, "Someone you're *never* going to know."

That made me sad. I moved away from him and rested my head against the door, staring out into the gathering dusk.

"I guess it bothers me," I admitted. "Having her locker and all. Maybe I feel . . . you know . . . connected to her in a way." I looked down and gave a sheepish laugh. "I know that sounds weird."

He didn't answer. He rested one elbow on the ledge of his open window and leaned his cheek against his palm.

"You really care about people, don't you?" He sounded slightly mystified. "That's so rare these days. Most people don't care about anything."

"Oh, please—"

"No, I mean it. Here's this girl you don't even know—I mean most of *us* hardly knew her—and you're . . . you know . . . concerned about her."

"It's just that . . ." I tried to find the right words, wanting to make him understand. "The whole thing seems so tragic to me. One of those horrible things you always read about that happens to someone else—except it happened to a *real person* who used to have my locker. And now . . . it's like she never even existed. But she *did* exist! She had a *life!*"

In the shadows I could feel his eyes upon my face, could feel the curious way they were watching me.

"Maybe you shouldn't think about it," he said at last. "It makes you too unhappy, and there's nothing you can do. It's been over for a long time."

"But it's *not* over, is it? Not really. Not till someone finds out what really happened to her."

"Most people have stopped wondering by now. They've gotten on with their lives."

"They might *not* have stopped wondering if she'd been from here." I sighed.

"But she wasn't," Tyler said. "She was an outsider."

"Is that how everyone's classified? You're either a townsfolk or an outsider?"

"Something like that, I guess." The idea seemed to amuse him. "Why? You afraid you're gonna get tarred and feathered and run out of town on a rail?"

"I'm beginning to worry."

I heard him laugh softly under his breath. He rearranged his cap in the same crooked position, and then he brushed absentmindedly at the hair blowing in his eyes. I sat there gazing at his profile and heard him say softly, "Quit looking at me."

"I'm not looking at you," I said, and he gave me a sidelong glance.

"Yes, you are."

Maybe it was because he sounded so self-conscious about it that I couldn't help teasing him.

"It's your smile," I said.

There was a long silence.

"Don't you want to know what I think about it?" I persisted.

"No."

"Well, I'm going to tell you anyway. It's a sweet smile. A wonderful smile. Sort of funny and whimsical—"

"Whimsical?"

"Yes, and kind of teasing and secretive and sly all at the same time." I hid a smile of my own as the silence dragged on and on. "It makes you look like a little boy," I finished.

"It does not."

"Yes, it most certainly does. Cute and shy. And vulnerable."

No answer.

I leaned over and put my face close to his. He was trying to keep his eyes on the road, but as I kept staring at his profile, pretending to study every feature, I saw a muscle move in his cheek, and he stole a glance at me.

"Are you blushing?" I whispered.

No response.

"Hmmm . . ." I mused. "I think maybe you are."

I could feel him squirm uncomfortably, and it was all I could do not to laugh.

"I told you you were shy." I couldn't help sounding smug.

His eyes shifted onto mine. That little smile played at the corners of his mouth.

"Stay close to me like that, and I'll show you how shy I am," Tyler said.

I stared at him.

I moved back.

I turned my face to the open window and let the cool air blow across my warm cheeks, and I heard Tyler laughing softly.

"Now who's blushing," he murmured.

The last shred of sunlight was finally slipping away. As we followed the road out of the trees, I could see a molten glow oozing over the hillsides, and the air smelled wet and earthy. Off in the distance I could see the ruins of a barn, rotting silently away in an empty field.

"Did Suellen really live back there in that awful place?" I asked quietly.

Tyler didn't answer right at first. He kept his eyes on the road ahead, slowing the car even more as we came to a steep incline.

"It wasn't always that bad," he said, shifting into low gear and starting the climb. "Out here it doesn't take long for nature to reclaim things, especially when nobody's using them anymore."

"Did you ever go out with her?"

The question popped out before I could stop it. I heard the words hanging in the air between us, but by then it was too late to do anything but feel like an idiot.

Tyler didn't look at me. His hands tightened on the steering wheel.

"Once," he said.

I waited for him to go on. He didn't.

Instead he coaxed the old car over the top of the hill, and then he leaned forward, squinting through the shadows and pointing to something I couldn't even see.

"Look—there's the bridge," he announced. "Welcome to Lost River."

7

The road came to an abrupt end.

Tyler stopped the car and jumped out, walking forward onto a rickety wooden bridge and pulling back a heavy chain with a sign on it that said PRIVATE.

"Where are we?" I asked him. We must have been riding for half an hour, at least. My ears were still ringing from the wind and the noisy engine, and I gingerly patted my head.

"We have a summer cabin down here," he informed me, hopping back in again. "My dad just wanted me to check on some things."

I craned my neck out the window as we drove slowly across the bridge. Broken boards sagged beneath the weight of the car, and in the glare of the headlights I could see what looked like a deep ravine yawning below. Shuddering a little, I drew back inside and watched as the dirt road sloped up a gentle rise, and wound through another stretch of woods, widening at last into a shadowy clearing, where it promptly dead-ended.

"That's our place," Tyler said.

I looked out at the small wooden cabin, its roof and porch and stone chimney practically swallowed by the surrounding trees. Dormer windows jutted out from the second floor, all of them heavily shuttered, and the encircling yard was tangled with weeds and dead leaves and fallen tree limbs.

"The Taj Mahal it's not," Tyler added. He stopped the car and turned off the ignition, glancing over at me with a shrug. "But we like it. Once we get it cleaned up for the summer, we spend lots of time here. It's a great place to bring friends. Lots of privacy."

He shoved open his door and climbed out, motioning me to follow.

"That's the river down there," he said, heading around to one side of the cabin. "It's high right now —we've had a lot of rain."

I could see now that the cabin was built at the top of an embankment. As Tyler walked to the edge, I came up behind him and gazed down into the muddy water below. A flight of wooden steps led down to a narrow dock, but I could hardly see it for all the overhanging trees. The place looked dark and spooky, and I pulled back nervously, all too conscious of the spongy ground underfoot.

"Be careful, it's slippery," Tyler warned me, reaching out for my hand. "You'd think we'd be safe here, wouldn't you, being up this far? But the truth is, a few good storms set in, and it's nothing for that water to come right over the bank. I've seen it flood so bad, we've had to leave the car way back down the road and paddle the boat in over the bridge."

I couldn't even picture the river rising this high. As Tyler let go of my hand and turned back toward the cabin, I lingered behind, taking another peek at the dock. The bank was matted with weeds and twisted clumps of tree roots, and as I stared, something slithered out of the shadows and into the murky water. Nervously I redirected my gaze to the middle of the river, where I could see a slow, lazy current swirling along. But down there along the bank the water didn't seem to be moving at all—just lying there deep and thick and stagnant . . .

Dead . . .

A chill crept up my arms.

Suddenly, more than anything else, I wanted to get back to the safety of the car.

I started to turn, and to my horror, felt my foot slipping in the mud. Panicking, I whirled around and gasped.

I hadn't heard Tyler come up behind me. I thought he'd gone into the cabin.

But now, as I locked eyes with him, I also felt something hit my arm, shoving me off balance.

I grabbed wildly for something—*anything*—to hold on to.

But there was only the wet ground dissolving beneath my shoes, and the shrill echo of my scream, and the endless rush of dank, dark air as I plunged into nothingness.

8

Marlee! Are you okay!"

I might have been out for a second or two—I'm not really sure. There was just that endless sensation of falling, and the bone-jarring impact, and then everything finally began to focus again, all blurs and slow motion.

I tried to move but couldn't. I felt like something was trapping me—something huge and alive—and sucking me down into a bottomless hole.

The first thing I saw clearly was Tyler sliding down the embankment after me, and I remember thinking in some weird corner of my mind that it was a miracle he was even staying on his feet at that crazy angle. The next thing I saw was his face above mine, and he looked scared to death.

"Marlee—can you hear me? Don't move!"

I wanted to tell him there was no danger at all of

that, I was stuck fast. But my immediate concern wasn't the weeds or the slime or even the throbbing in my head, it was suddenly remembering that slithery thing I'd seen earlier.

"Get me out of here!" I yelled. "I think I saw a snake!"

"If you did, he never knew what hit him. Hang on—your foot's caught."

I tried to lift myself up, but only sank back helplessly into the muck. I could feel Tyler's fingers around my ankle, and as a terrible pressure suddenly disappeared, I saw him grin triumphantly and toss my sneaker into the water.

"What are you doing to my shoe?" I cried, but his arms were around me now, tugging me to my feet. "I *need* that shoe!"

"Forget the shoe. Can you stand up?" He loosened his hold on me, and I started to crumple. "Negative on standing. Maybe something's broken after all."

I winced and shook my head. "I'm sorry. I'll try harder—"

And then it happened.

Just like before—only this time I was right in the middle of it—*trapped* in the middle of it—like suddenly finding myself in a movie scene, but not being able to get out because the film's running on fast forward and no one can stop it—

Panic . . . terror . . . pain pain pain bursting exploding darkness surging in swallowing me—something else—a smell again—only different this time—thick . . . clinging . . . suffocating wet slippery can't breathe . . . oh, God, can't breathe, what is it—

"It's murder," Tyler was saying.

"Wh-what?" I whispered.

"I said it's *murder* coming down that way. Next time I wish you'd use the steps."

I looked at him in dismay. I was standing up clutching the top of my head, and Tyler was still holding me. I was shaking all over, but I was also testing my weight on one foot, and everything was sharply back in focus. I was pressed up against his chest, and we were both covered in mud, and as I looked up into his face, a flash of memory came back to me—*something hit my arm . . . his eyes were so dark . . . I didn't know he was there . . .*

"You okay?" Tyler asked. "Did you hurt your head?"

"You—" I broke off, suddenly confused. Anger and fear and pain roared through me, and I pulled back, pushing him away. "Something . . . something hit me."

"Did it?" Tyler's face was blank. "I saw you slipping, and I couldn't believe it. I tried to get to you —tried to *grab* you, but you were already on your way down."

I stared at him. His clothes were filthy and torn, and there were streaks of dirt on his face. He ran a hand over one cheek, making it even worse.

"Something pushed me," I mumbled, and I took another step back.

"You slipped," he said quietly.

I looked up into his eyes. He held my gaze with a steady one of his own, and with an effort I turned my attention to the riverbank.

"You can't get up the same way you came down," he deadpanned. "Here. Hold on to me."

"I can do it myself," I said.

He didn't argue, only reached over and took my hand, leading the way carefully through the tall grass until he was able to touch the stairs with one shoe. Then, digging in his heels, he gave me an encouraging nod and pulled gently, guiding me to solid ground. Relieved, I felt the steps beneath my feet and Tyler's hands around my waist, boosting me up. I tried to pretend I didn't notice anything, but a curious tingle went through me, and I ended up stumbling.

"You're okay," he said, catching my elbow, steering me again. "I'm right behind you."

I didn't want him to be right behind me. I especially didn't want him right behind me when I knew my rear end was wet and covered with mud and grass stains.

"I hope we can fix this big rip back here," he said.

I whirled around, and he sucked in both his cheeks, making his face clownishly solemn.

"Joke," he said, holding up one hand. "Really. I swear."

I was so glad to get to the cabin. While Tyler unlocked the door, I stood behind him, watching his quick, deft movements. I tried to remember exactly what had happened back there on the riverbank . . . what had happened the second before I fell . . . *but Tyler said I was already falling when he grabbed for me . . . I must have felt him trying to catch me, but he missed. . . .*

"Are *my* jeans ripped?" Tyler asked, and I snapped

back to attention. He was looking down at himself and frowning.

"Sorry. What?"

"You're undressing me with your eyes," he said.

"I most certainly am not."

"Come on, you know you were." He winked and stepped aside to hold open the door. "After you."

The cabin was surprisingly homey. At one end was a huge kitchen with a big oak table, and at the other end a cozy living room, one wall taken up by a stone fireplace. The floors were all wood, the walls paneled, and every window had a view of the trees. A wide porch stretched across the entire rear of the cabin, and when Tyler opened the back door, I could see the forest pressing right up to the steps. In one corner of the kitchen an open staircase led to the second story, where Tyler showed me the huge room full of beds and mismatched furniture.

"As you can see, my mom's big on hospitality." He shrugged. "Everyone comes here to crash, so we always have plenty of sleeping space."

"It's nice," I told him. My arm was starting to hurt, and I rubbed distractedly at the torn sleeve. "Do you ever come here by yourself? Just to be alone and think?"

"Actually, it's the best place in the world when nobody else is here. And since you and I are neighbors now, if you ever want to come and be alone and think, be my guest."

"What about your parents? Won't they mind?"

"Of course not." He looked surprised. "They both

work during the week, and my mom babysits a lot, so she's usually busy on the weekends. Come anytime you want. I'll even show you where we hide the key."

I couldn't help smiling at the offer. "That's really nice of you. You don't even know me."

"What does that mean?" he teased. "Is there something I *should* know?"

I shook my head. "Not really."

"Like . . . are you an ax murderer? A psychopath? A reform-school escapee?"

Again I shook my head, but this time I was laughing. "No. None of the above."

"Well"—he looked me slowly up and down—"you never can tell about people. You *seem* harmless enough, but you can't be too careful these days."

I started to nod, started to say something clever, but Tyler went over to an old dresser and began rummaging through its drawers.

"Here," he said, tossing me a bundle of clothes.

"What's this?"

"What do you mean, what's this?" he scolded gently. "Look at you, you're a mess. Put these dry things on before you catch pneumonia."

I hesitated, staring down at the clothes in my hands. Tyler went back down the stairs, and a second later I heard him whistling as he opened and shut cabinet doors. I kept one eye on the stairs and cautiously began to undress.

"People break in sometimes!" Tyler's voice floated up the stairs, and I moved closer, trying to hear.

"What did you say?"

"I said, people break in sometimes! Into the cabins! All up and down the river!"

"Is that why we're here?"

"Sort of. Jimmy Frank called my dad about changing the locks before we start leaving stuff down here for the summer. We've had stuff stolen before."

"Like what?"

"Oh . . . radios. Tools. Fishing tackle . . . things like that. Most of the time it's not worth much, but last year we lost a boat motor and some of my dad's guns."

I pulled on a baggy pair of jeans and frowned as the legs billowed out around me. I slipped into the huge shirt and decided both things must belong to Tyler's father.

"Are you finding anything suspicious?" I called back, sliding into dry socks.

"Usually when there's been a break-in, it's just transients, looking for food and a dry place to spend the night—especially if the weather's bad!"

Rattles, crashes, more bangs. Doors opening and closing. Windows being raised and lowered.

"Everything looks okay to me," Tyler announced.

"Who's Jimmy Frank?" I called to him, rolling my wet things together into a ball.

"The caretaker. People only use these cabins in the summer. Jimmy Frank does anything that needs doing—repairs, maintenance, stuff like that. But last year, with the robberies and all, folks asked him to keep an eye on things during the off-season. Haven't you met him yet?"

"Why would I?"

"He goes to school with us. You must have seen him in class."

Tyler didn't hear me slip downstairs. I stood there watching as he climbed up on the back of the couch to check the lock on a window. His jeans were still wet, molded tight to his narrow hips, and he'd taken his shoes off and stripped to his T-shirt. His head was angled slightly back, and his hair swished back and forth across his shoulder blades like a soft black cloud. *What's the matter with you, are you crazy? What possible reason would he have for pushing you down a hill?*

While I hesitated there at the bottom of the steps, Tyler turned and saw me, his face exploding in a giant grin.

"Wow! You look like a clown!"

"Thanks," I grumbled.

"A cute one, though. I meant a really *cute* clown."

"Are these your dad's?" I said irritably. *Great way to make an impression, Marlee. I'm sure you'll be engraved in his memory forever and ever.*

"Actually they're my older brother Eugene's," Tyler said. "He's really fat, so he ran away from home last year and joined a traveling sideshow."

I narrowed my eyes at him. "Is that true?"

"Of course it isn't true." He gave me a chiding look and hopped back down onto the floor. "I don't even have a brother named Eugene. Well, I can't find a single thing going on here. I guess we'd better get back."

"Can I do anything?"

"Just wait in the car while I lock up."

Dusk had turned to full dark by now. As I sat there alone waiting for Tyler to come back, I could hear all these weird whispery sounds around me . . . invisible things moving through the shadows, camouflaged by the night. I wrapped my arms tight around myself and fought off a bad case of nerves. Far below me the river flowed, and an owl hooted mournfully, and the wind sighed through the trees, making them bend and sway like zombies on the loose.

Now, why did I think of that? Why zombies?

"Tyler?" I called.

"Yeah! Coming!"

He stepped out onto the porch and locked the door behind him. I finally began to relax a little when we were well on our way down the road.

"Did you find anything?" I asked him as he fiddled with the radio.

The light was so dim inside the car, I could barely see him shaking his head.

"No. If anyone *was* there, they didn't bother anything."

I nodded and leaned back into the seat. "Why do they call it Lost River?"

For one instant Tyler's hand was caught in the glow of the dashboard. It paused in midair as though frozen.

"Because," he said slowly, "it's so deep and the undercurrents are so strong."

The radio sputtered with static. Tyler clicked it off.

"It's a spooky name," I murmured.

"It's a spooky river," Tyler replied. He thought a

moment, then went on. "It winds back through those woods where the sun can't even reach. People've been known to get lost back there . . . some never come out again. And those that do come out . . ."

His voice trailed off. I stared at his shadowy silhouette, knowing he couldn't see me now in the dark.

"Those that do, what?" I coaxed.

"Oh, you know how rumors are." He brushed off my question, yet his voice sounded tight, and his shoulders seemed to have stiffened. "Some say the river's possessed. That it calls to you, and when you hear it, all you want to do is be a part of it forever. And all the souls of the ones who've drowned, they beckon new ones to join them."

A heavy silence fell.

I could hear my heartbeat quickening and the rush of the wind through the car and the chirping of crickets from the darkness. I took a deep breath and swallowed hard.

"Sorry I asked. Just what I needed to help me sleep tonight."

"But you don't really believe any of that, do you?" His voice was low. "Haven't you been warned about small-town gossip? For each story someone tells, there's always someone else trying to top it."

And suddenly he laughed—a quick, nervous sound in the uneasy quiet.

I tried to laugh, too, but couldn't.

I turned my face to the window and let the deep, dark night flow over me, and wondered why I suddenly felt so cold.

9

It's funny how morning can give everything a fresh new perspective.

When I woke up the next day and saw the sun shining and heard the sparrows singing outside my window, all the scary things that had upset me before seemed like a bad dream. I even stared at my reflection in the bathroom mirror and gave myself a good talking to before I went down to breakfast.

"Small-town gossip," I told myself sternly. "Small-town gossip and a bad case of new-school jitters. Nothing strange is going on in your life. So remember that and be sensible for a change."

"You're fooling yourself." Dobkin frowned at me from the hall. "You know as well as I do that something strange is going on."

"I don't know anything of the sort."

71

"Well"—he sighed in his most tolerant manner—"since you're being so stubborn about it, at least take these with you."

Frowning, I turned to see him holding something in his hands.

"What are those?"

"Magic charms," he explained. "Hang these in your locker. Maybe they'll help."

I stared down at the items he'd given me. A small mirror. A bent-up photo of him and Aunt Celia and me on the beach. A plain three-by-five index card with a message printed in a childish hand: SUELLEN DOESN'T LIVE HERE ANYMORE.

"What in the world is this?" I waved the card under his nose.

"Kind of like a spell," he said gravely. "So any spirits hanging around will go away."

"You go away." I slammed the door in his face and gritted my teeth, more determined than ever to have a wonderful day.

Noreen was waiting for me by the steps when I got to school, and I yelled and waved to her, barely even acknowledging Dobkin as I jumped out of the van. He'd been lecturing me under his breath all the way there, and as I glanced back at him, he shook his head in that resigned way he has when he knows he's right and I'm going to be sorry I didn't listen to him. Noreen led the way into the building, chattering nonstop about some paper she was supposed to turn in today but didn't have the faintest idea what it was supposed to be about, and that's why she'd forgotten to write it. I was so busy listening to her that I didn't realize someone had come up behind me until I felt a tap on my shoulder.

"Hey," Tyler said, just loud enough for Noreen to hear. "You forgot your clothes."

Beside me Noreen braked to a halt, and we both spun around to face him. He was holding out his hands, and I recognized the filthy jeans and shirt I'd been wearing yesterday. As I stared down at them, I felt my cheeks go beet red.

"Wow!" Somehow Noreen managed to keep a straight face. "Is there something I should know about?"

A faint smile played over Tyler's lips, and he shook his head mysteriously.

"Our secret," he whispered. He dropped my clothes on my armload of books and moved out into the flow of students rushing to class. I opened my mouth to yell at him, but he'd already disappeared.

"It's not what you think," I stammered, but Noreen only hooted with laughter and linked her arm through mine.

"Come on, I know Tyler. Shall I help you kill him *now* or *later?*"

"He showed me his family's cabin last night." I felt like I had to say something to explain, so I rushed on. "I tripped and fell and rolled right down the riverbank. Definitely one of my more graceful moments."

The picture I painted was enough to send her into fresh peals of laughter. Kids at the other end of the hall actually craned their necks to see what they were missing.

"He was so nice about it," I added, remembering.

"Come to think of it, he *could* have taken the steps down to help me, but instead he just came sliding down in the mud."

Noreen and I looked at each other.

"I think he was trying to be polite," I said.

At this we both exploded into giggles. Students hurrying past gave us weird looks, and we pressed back against the wall, trying to get ourselves under control.

"He's not like anyone else in the world." Noreen caught her breath at last and rubbed tears from her eyes. "I remember as far back as kindergarten, he was always just a little out of sync with the rest of the human race." Her face screwed up in deep thought, and then she added, "He's totally unpredictable. In fact, that's the only thing *predictable* about him—is that he's *un*predictable."

We started walking again, and Noreen sighed, throwing me an amused look.

"You know, when I was little, I used to think Tyler was an alien? No, *really!*"

Again we burst into laughter, taking several more minutes of concentrated effort to finally quiet down.

"I *believed* he was an alien," Noreen went on breathlessly, "and I kept waiting and waiting for him to show me his spaceship, and I wanted so *bad* to go off with him to some other planet." She gave a wistful sigh. "I figured it had to be the most fun planet in the whole universe if Tyler was from there."

We rounded the corner, and suddenly I stopped, taking her arm.

"Look, Noreen, who's that?"

"Where?"

"There. That guy standing next to my locker."

"Oh, him?" She raked one hand through her curls in a nervous sort of way. "That's Jimmy Frank Baldwin. Why?"

I shook my head, watching as he shoved some books inside, stepped back and closed his locker door.

"I don't think he likes me."

"Why not?" Noreen's glance flicked between me and Jimmy Frank and she frowned. "Does he even know you?"

Shaking my head, I said, "It's just his attitude. We were both at our lockers yesterday, and I thought he was kind of rude. You know . . . making assumptions about me that weren't even true."

"Yeah," she sighed, "he's not exactly known for his tact. He's kind of a loner—doesn't like outsiders much. But who cares about attitude when someone's that gorgeous, right?" She rolled her eyes wistfully, clasping her books to her chest. "His dad's the sheriff here, but they have a farm out on Dry Creek Road. Jimmy Frank spends most of his time keeping an eye on those cabins along Lost River. He's kind of the caretaker."

"Which is why you like to visit Tyler's cabin." I nodded. *"Now* I'm beginning to understand . . ."

"Lot of good it does me." Noreen sniffed. "Do you realize I've known Jimmy Frank *almost* as long as I've known Tyler—and he *still* has absolutely *no* idea of the depth of my lust. Maybe," she added thoughtfully, "I could fall out of a boat next time I'm there. Or a window. Or . . . my swimsuit."

We burst out laughing again, and when we did, Jimmy Frank's head came up sharply, his narrowed eyes shooting straight across the hallway and onto me. I immediately looked away, but Noreen walked straight over.

"Hey!" She grinned. "Jimmy Frank! Have you met my friend Marlee?"

I was mortified. As I tried to pull out of her grasp, Noreen pulled just as stubbornly on my arm, forcing me across the hall to where Jimmy Frank waited and stared.

"She's from Florida," Noreen chattered on. "She just started school here yesterday. Did you know she's renting—"

"The old Turley place," he cut her off. "I heard." His blue-green eyes swept over me with deliberate insolence. "And yes, we've already met."

"Just checking." Noreen gave him her most dazzling smile. "Wouldn't want anyone to miss out on the introductions."

Jimmy Frank slammed his locker door, but his eyes were still on me, and they were making me very nervous.

"I've got to get my stuff," I mumbled, and Noreen nodded, finally letting me go, but giving her full attention to Jimmy Frank.

I twirled the dial on my lock, juggling my books from one arm to the other. Behind me I could hear Noreen going on again about that English paper that was due, and Jimmy Frank was answering her in a monotone that reminded me of Dobkin's when he wished I'd just get lost and quit bothering him.

The lock clicked apart, and for a long moment I just stood there looking at it, thinking back to yesterday morning. *But nothing happened yesterday afternoon when I came to my locker. . . . There's no reason to think anything will happen now or ever again.*

Taking a deep breath, I yanked the door open with such force that Noreen and Jimmy Frank quit talking to each other and turned to stare at me.

"Sorry," I mumbled.

I was fidgeting so bad, I dropped one of my books, and when I leaned down to pick it up, two more fell out of my arms. Noreen and Jimmy Frank both bent down to help, and I bit my lip in frustration.

"Sorry," I said again. "I'm so clumsy this morning."

"Clumsy?" Jimmy Frank echoed, and I could swear there was a touch of sarcasm in his voice.

He straightened up and held out my book. I tried to take it from him, but his fingers tightened on the cover, and his eyes locked with mine.

"What are you so nervous about, Marlee?" he whispered.

"Hey, your face is enough to make anyone nervous," Noreen shot back, nodding at me to hurry. "Didn't I see you yesterday, Jimmy Frank? Standing out in the middle of a cornfield with crows on your arms?"

He said something back to her, but I didn't hear. I was too busy cramming my books in my locker and trying to pull out the other stuff I needed.

"You go on," I said to Noreen. "I'll meet you in homeroom."

Noreen looked reluctant to leave me. "You remember where to go?"

"Sure, I'll only be a minute. There's no point in holding you up."

Luckily Jimmy Frank turned to go; otherwise I think Noreen would have stayed right there with me. As it was, she hurried after him, and I heard her talking all the way down the hall until they both turned a corner and disappeared. Only then did I take a deep breath and face my locker again.

Nice and normal. No ghosts here.

I glanced up at the hall clock and saw that I still had a few minutes before the bell rang. Then I glanced around to make sure no one was paying attention to me. And then I dug into my purse and pulled out the mirror, the photo, and the index card that Dobkin had given me. *I can't believe I'm doing this.* . . . And yet I stood right there with my little roll of tape and slapped the photo and the card up in my locker, and hung the mirror from a string I stuck to the back of the door. *There, that should do it. God, what an idiot!*

The bell rang, nearly sending me out of my skin. I grabbed one of my notebooks and glanced back over my shoulder.

That's funny . . . just a minute ago there were other people in the hall. . . .

But not now.

In fact, as I stood there looking around me, it was like everything had totally disappeared in the space of a second—as if somehow I'd only dreamed coming to school this morning, walking with Noreen, opening my locker door . . .

THE LOCKER

Where's that chill coming from?

Giving an involuntary shiver, I stepped back and looked up both ends of the deserted corridor, trying to see if an outside door had been left open by mistake. It hadn't been this cold when I'd come to school only half an hour ago, but now the hallway was absolutely freezing. I could feel it raising hairs along the back of my neck and making little drafts around my feet—not just a breeze, but something much more forceful.

Really nervous now, I turned back to my locker and reached for my math book on the very bottom of the stack. I pulled on it, but it wouldn't budge. I pulled again, but it might as well have been glued to the shelf.

"What's wrong with this stupid thing?"

I was muttering to myself and tugging for all I was worth, and in the back of my mind I could feel my fingers getting colder and colder until they were almost too cold to work anymore. Thoroughly frustrated now, I held them to my lips and blew on them, and then I rubbed my palms together and blew on them again.

"This is *crazy!* What is going *on* around here?"

Giving a final heave, I felt the book come loose at last, and as I stepped back to catch myself, I happened to look up at the mirror on my locker door.

I looked . . .

And I looked . . .

And I felt a scream come up in my throat like a frozen lump of terror.

At first it was my own face I saw reflected there.

But then it began to fade . . .

To disappear . . .

79

And another one took its place, staring back at me, blurry and indistinct—like a watercolor portrait not quite dry, its mournful expression smeared and dripping and running together in tiny streams of brown and dark, dark red. . . .

The eyes were dull and vacant.

The mouth gaped wide.

And as I began to choke, sucking a strange coppery odor deep into my lungs, I was suddenly and violently aware of two things:

The dark, dark red was blood.

And the face staring back at me was dead.

10

I don't know when it ended.

I don't know how long I stood there or how long I gazed at that hideous face.

It was probably only seconds, but it seemed like hours.

I only knew that some piercing sound was drilling into my brain, and as I finally blinked my eyes and made a strangled sound in my throat, someone grabbed my arm and spun me around.

"What is it?" Jimmy Frank demanded. His fingers dug hard into my flesh, and I couldn't pull away. "What's the matter with you? Why were you screaming?"

"The—the mirror!" I stammered. "Stop! You're hurting me—"

"What mirror? What are you talking about?"

"There's something wrong with my locker! Can't you see it—can't—"

"So they aren't rumors after all." His eyes narrowed, and his voice sank low. "Something really *did* happen yesterday, didn't it?"

"Marlee! Hey, Marlee, what's going on?"

Jimmy Frank's hands fell away as Tyler ran up behind him. Through a strange sort of fog I saw the puzzled look on Tyler's face, saw him glance at Jimmy Frank and then back at me. And then, as I came fully to my senses, I also saw that the hall was swarming with kids, and that a lot of them were bunched up in little groups, whispering and staring at me. I wanted to die.

"Where was everyone?" I asked stupidly. I put one hand to my forehead and asked again. "Where was everyone a minute ago? Why wasn't there anyone else in the hall?"

"They were all in homeroom," Tyler informed me. "Where you should have been."

Jimmy Frank's eyes were glued to my face. He squeezed one hand into a fist. He raised it slowly up to my locker, and hit the door, slamming it shut.

"Didn't you hear the bell?" Tyler asked.

"Yes, *this* bell—" I was trying to think, but there were too many blank spots in my mind. "Not the bell for homeroom. . . . It wasn't time for homeroom when I . . ."

I looked helplessly at Tyler, who leaned back against the wall, took a yo-yo from his shirt pocket, and swung it lazily down to the floor. It recoiled into his hand, and he sent it down again . . . up . . . down . . . up . . . down. One by one, the kids who'd been watching us began to wander back into the general chaos of the hall.

"It was the mirror," I said at last, and though Tyler raised an eyebrow, he didn't look up from his toy.

"What mirror?" he asked.

"Inside my locker. Just look for yourself—it's horrible."

This time Tyler straightened up. He tucked his yo-yo away and flashed me a look of such total bewilderment that I might have laughed if I hadn't been so terrified.

"Just what we need around here," Jimmy Frank muttered. "A brand-new wave of hysterics."

Tyler shrugged and nodded. The two of them crowded close to my locker, opened the door, and looked in.

"I see the mirror," Tyler said softly.

"And who's *in* the mirror?" I could barely get the words out.

There was a long, long silence. I put one hand to my forehead, suddenly afraid I might faint.

Tyler sounded apologetic. "We are."

I stared at him. I stared at Jimmy Frank. Then I crept up between them and slowly craned my head till I could see my own reflection sandwiched in with theirs.

"Someone was in the mirror," I mumbled. When neither of them answered, my voice rose defensively. "Someone *was* there! And it wasn't me!"

Jimmy Frank swore under his breath and turned back to his locker. "I'm not gonna be late on account of some loonytune."

"He means you," Tyler explained. "Come on. We've got to get to class."

"*You* believe me, don't you?" I asked, gathering my stuff and following him. The desperation in my voice embarrassed me. "I'm *not* making it up—I'm *not* imagining it!"

"Hey"—Tyler turned toward me and walked backward, nodding his head emphatically—"I believe in everything."

"I know what you're thinking," I went on, following him, not even sure he was listening anymore because now he had his back to me again. "You're thinking I have bad eyes or—or—maybe somebody came up behind me in the hall and I didn't hear them, but it wasn't like that. It wasn't like that at all. This thing—this person in my mirror—it was—*she* was—"

"She?" Tyler glanced back but kept moving. "You said 'she.' How come?"

"I don't know," I said truthfully. "I don't know why I said 'she'—it just *seemed* like a she—"

"And you *also* said," Tyler scolded, walking backward again, shaking his finger at me, "that you weren't crazy like old lady Turley. Were you lying to me?"

"I said I *might* be," I threw back at him, not really appreciating the teasing. "But the truth is, I'm *not.*"

He opened his eyes wide and gave a slow, solemn nod. "Um-hmmm . . . and I *believe* you—"

"Will you stop it and just listen a minute?" I burst out. "She wasn't real! I—I can't explain it exactly, but the face in the mirror was all wavy and blurry, and it was like *her* face was superimposed on *mine!* Like a *dream*—only I was wide awake! It was horrible—I couldn't stand the way she was looking at me!"

"Well, you've got everyone else looking at you now," Tyler mumbled out one side of his mouth. "Keep your voice down." He took my arm and hustled me quickly through the hall, greeting each curious stare with a smile and a nod. "Hello there. Hello . . . hello . . ."

"I'm not crazy," I said furiously as we rounded a corner and I broke free of his grasp. Tyler stepped back and threw his hands in the air.

"Would *I* know the difference?"

I stared at him. My mind was going in circles so fast that I couldn't think . . . couldn't focus . . . couldn't make sense of anything. After a long while I finally nodded. "You're right," I said, trying to be calm. "I don't know what's been happening to me, but there has to be a logical explanation for it." When Tyler didn't say anything, my voice rose again. "Do you have any idea how upsetting this all is? How embarrassing?"

I ducked my head, suddenly afraid I might start to cry. I felt Tyler's arm slip gently around my shoulders . . . felt his lips move close to my ear.

"I'm sorry," he whispered.

I didn't want anyone to see us like that, and yet part of me wanted to just stand there and have him close to me forever. I felt scared and all mixed up, and it was a relief to finally get to class, though I can't tell you a single thing that went on the rest of the morning.

At least . . . not till lunchtime.

I left the building fast, pretty sure that everyone had heard about my second big locker fiasco by now. I couldn't stand the thought of being stared at and laughed at, so I took off down the sidewalk to the kindergarten, suddenly wanting more than anything to see Dobkin. Funny how his and my minds have always worked together at times of great crisis—no sooner had I left the campus and gotten halfway down the block than I saw his blond head bobbing toward me from the opposite direction.

"How did you get out?" I greeted him. "I thought it was against the rules."

"What can they do—expell me?" He shrugged. "And who's gonna miss me with a hundred other kids taking naps?" He thought a minute, cocked his head at me, and added, "I stuffed my sleeping bag with some teddy bears. They'll never know."

"Genius." I ruffled his hair, and though he grimaced, deep down I knew he was pleased.

"So what prompted this great meeting of the minds?" I asked casually.

"Why don't you tell me?" he countered.

I could see a sheaf of papers under his arm, and as each of us waited for the other to start, I spotted an empty bench at the corner bus stop, and we sat down.

"Here," Dobkin said proudly, "is all the information I could find on Suellen Downing."

My mouth fell open. Even though I tell myself that Dobkin can never do another thing to amaze me, still he always manages to do it.

"Where on earth did you get these?" I demanded,

opening the folder he handed me, flipping quickly through a stack of photocopies.

He shrugged. "Library."

"But how—"

"They took us there on a field trip this morning." The look on his face clearly showed what he thought about that. "And so I told the librarian my sister was doing a paper on unsolved mysteries. She brought up the subject of Suellen Downing, and the rest was easy."

"In other words, you charmed her," I said, and he gave a modest nod.

"Those are all the articles from local papers," Dobkin went on. "Maybe something will seem familiar."

But something already had.

As I stared down at the first streaked copy, I could feel my blood chilling in my veins.

"That's her," I croaked.

Dobkin leaned across me to see. "Her picture, yeah. So what?"

My shoulders sagged, and my breath came out in a shallow rush.

"That's the girl in my mirror," I whispered.

11

Of course Dobkin didn't have the faintest idea what I was talking about. We sat there side by side on the bench while I told him what had happened at my locker that morning, and the whole time I talked, he just stared down at his sneakers, his hands clasped together on his stomach, nodding his head like some wise little Buddha who was biting his tongue to keep from saying "I told you so."

"That's the girl," I said again when my story was finished. I felt drained. Worse than drained.

"You're sure?"

Slowly I nodded. "The image—whatever it was— was blurry and faded, but I'd know the face anywhere." I put my hands over my eyes and moaned. "Oh, God . . ."

"She's dead, isn't she?" Dobkin murmured, and I glanced at him sadly.

"Yes. She is."

"You sure?" He wanted me to be wrong, but I knew deep in my heart that I wasn't.

"Then you'll have to find out where she is," Dobkin said. "And what happened to her."

"Are you out of your—"

"You have to, Marlee. You have to so her family will know. So they can go get her and . . . and bring her home again."

And suddenly he wasn't the philosopher anymore, but only a very little boy, trying desperately not to cry, and I put my arms around him and held him because there was no Mom and Dad to do it in my place.

We know about losing people, Dobkin and I.

"You better get back to school." I made my voice stern because I knew he'd bristle at that, and it would take his mind off being sad. At that moment we both saw Aunt Celia's van flying past us in the street on its way to the kindergarten, and we looked at each other and sighed.

"Trouble *big* time, Bud," I said sympathetically, and he nodded. "Want me to go with you?"

His glance was scathing. "I'll tell them I was trying to find the bathroom and got lost."

"Give me the look," I said, and his face collapsed into such a pitiful, scared expression, that it was all I could do to keep from laughing. "That should do it," I agreed, and I stood there and waited till he turned in through his schoolyard gate.

Back at my own school I found a nice tree behind the main building and sat down underneath it to think. I knew I wouldn't be able to avoid people forever—or their comments—or their questions— and that terrified me. Here I was, the new kid—the *outsider*—coming in and having weird experiences over some girl who'd mysteriously disappeared. And all because I'd been lucky enough to get her stupid locker.

Remembering the face in the mirror, I felt a deep, cold tremor go through me. *Suellen . . . can you hear me? That was blood, wasn't it? Which means . . . you either killed yourself . . . had a tragic accident . . . or were—*

"Marlee, are you okay?"

The voice was so close to me that I jumped and gave a little scream. Noreen stepped quickly away, then dropped to her knees beside me.

"I didn't mean to scare you! Oh, gosh, are you all right?"

"Sorry," I breathed. "I didn't even hear you."

"Would you rather be by yourself?" Her face wrinkled up in concern. "You know . . . I'm here if you want to talk."

Of course I wanted to talk. But what could I possibly say that wouldn't sound absolutely insane? I had to go to school here . . . I had to see these kids every day as long as we stayed in Edison. . . .

"No," I said finally and sighed. "But thanks for offering. That means a lot."

"I was talking to Tyler, and he told me what happened," she went on, dropping her eyes like she didn't want to embarrass me.

"I'm sure *everyone* knows about it," I said glumly,

feeling even worse when she gave a hesitant nod. "I'll be avoided like the plague."

"No, you won't." She moved over and put her arm around my shoulder, giving me a reassuring squeeze. "Of course that won't happen. Once people get to know you, they won't even remember this locker stuff. And anyway, you have me. And Tyler," she added, grinning. "Speaking of plagues."

I smiled a little, but it didn't last long.

"What are people saying?" I confronted her, noticing how she drew back a little at my question.

"What do you mean?"

"You know. About my locker. The things going on. What are people saying about it? I know you've heard something."

She looked like she really didn't want to get into it, and she tried to laugh it off.

"*You* know what they're saying." She rolled her eyes and gave a high-pitched laugh. "Just what you'd expect them to say. That the locker's haunted. You know. Stupid things like that."

I stared at her. "Did they say that before I got here? Or just since I've been here?"

Now she looked really uncomfortable.

"Well . . . you know how kids are . . . how stuff like that gets started when there's some kind of unexplained tragedy."

"So you knew I was getting a haunted locker, and you didn't tell me."

"Well, what was I supposed to say?" Noreen defended herself. "It's just stupid stuff kids make up!

Nobody *really* believes it! And how would you have taken it if I *had* told you? You'd have laughed yourself silly and thought *I* was crazy!"

I stared at her a minute. She bit her lip and looked away, and then she looked straight back at me.

"Well, you would have! You *know* you would have!"

I didn't know how to respond to that. So instead I burst out laughing, and after a few seconds Noreen laughed, too. In fact we laughed and laughed so hard that my sides hurt by the time we finally stopped.

"Welcome to Edison High." Noreen sighed, wiping her eyes. "Oh, and by the way, here's your locker, and I hope you don't mind if it's haunted. Geez . . ."

"Why do kids *say* it's haunted?" I wanted to know.

"Well, maybe *haunted* isn't the right word," she tried to explain to me. "Maybe it's just more—you know—superstition. I mean, the girl who had it disappeared. So of course *nobody* wants to use her locker. Like you could catch bad luck from touching anything that belonged to her."

She thought a minute, then laughed again.

"And the jokes. Sick ones, you know the type. 'Oh, sorry I don't have that homework assignment—I walked by Suellen's locker and it disappeared!' Dumb stuff like that."

I mulled all this over, casting her a sidelong glance. "And you really think it's all stupid? You don't believe the locker's really haunted?"

"Of course not! I don't believe in any of that stuff. And anyway"—she glanced down, concentrating on some grass she was twisting around her fingers— "why would it suddenly start being really and truly haunted now when it's been sitting there empty all this time?"

"Maybe because the right person came along to use it," a voice said, and we both gasped and looked up.

Jimmy Frank was standing over us, his face set and hard. I could see his hands at his sides, clenched into fists, and as his eyes moved slowly over us, his mouth moved in a kind of sneer.

"What do you mean, the right person?" Noreen came to my defense, chattering on like a magpie. "She's the *only* person to come here and use it. What a dumb thing to say."

"It's not dumb at all," he said, and to my surprise, he squatted down on his heels beside us and looked right into my eyes. "It's sort of like . . . psychometry. Isn't it, Marlee?"

I knew what he was talking about, all right.

As he said it out loud and continued to look at me, I felt my stomach churn, and I prayed I wouldn't get sick all over myself and them, too.

"What's the matter with you?" Noreen asked, glaring into Jimmy Frank's face. "I don't even know what you're talking about—that big word you just used. Get out of here. Can't you see we're having a private talk?"

"About what?" he persisted. "Suellen?"

"Come on." Noreen reached out and gave him a swat on his arm, sort of like a fly trying to intimidate an elephant. "Leave us alone."

"It's a form of ESP, isn't it?" Jimmy Frank went on conversationally, but there was no pleasantness in his eyes. "Only you use it to read particular objects."

"Hey, Tyler," Noreen called, exasperated. "Will you guys please just get out of here and leave us alone?"

I hadn't noticed Tyler standing off a little ways, but now he sauntered up, hands in pockets, eyes wide with interest.

"Psycho—what?" he asked, and Noreen groaned.

"Psychometry," Jimmy Frank stated. "A person can hold something in his hands, and it gives off information."

"What kind?" Tyler prodded him with the toe of one shoe.

"All kinds." Jimmy Frank was answering Tyler, but he hadn't taken his eyes off me. "Like certain people . . . and certain circumstances connected with the object."

Beside me Noreen gave a noticeable shudder. "Ooh, that's creepy. You're making Marlee sound like some kind of fortune-teller. Or witch."

"How do you know so much about it anyway?" Tyler demanded. "You hold a cowpie out on your farm, you can tell which cow did it?"

Noreen shrieked with laughter, and Tyler looked immensely pleased with himself. Any other time I might have found it funny, too, but not now—not with the way Jimmy Frank was pinning me with his eyes.

"It's true." He shrugged his broad shoulders and stood up again. "Just 'cause you haven't heard of it doesn't mean it can't happen."

"Here, Marlee, read this." Noreen giggled, digging in her purse and shoving her pen into my hand. "I used it to write the answers to my history test—do you think I got an A?"

"Put your hand on Noreen's head," Tyler deadpanned. "You won't know *anything*." He grabbed an overhead branch with both hands and swung gracefully back and forth till Noreen dived at him and tickled him, making him drop.

"You know, Jimmy Frank, with people like you around here, no wonder Marlee feels sick all the time," Noreen said shortly, pulling Tyler back onto his feet. She brushed fiercely at the back of his jeans, but when Tyler gave her a deliberately suggestive smile, she stopped and shoved him. "It's hard enough coming into a strange new place where you don't know anybody, without people accusing you of dumb things. And anyway, Marlee didn't *hold* the locker in her hands—a locker's too *big* to hold in your hands— so she can't even *use* this psycho-whatever it is if she can't *hold* something in her hands. She's probably just coming down with the flu or something, and you're gonna have everyone treating her like she's some kind of weirdo."

It was loyal of Noreen, and I appreciated it. Yet as she sat back down again and rested one hand on the file folder Dobkin had given me, it was all I could do not to scream and push her away.

"I'm not accusing her," Jimmy Frank said smoothly. He shook his head at Noreen and folded his arms across his chest. "Did I say she was doing anything weird? Sometimes people don't even *know* they're psychic. I just wondered if she'd ever heard of it, that's all."

Noreen patted the folder impatiently. She picked it up and waved it at him, shooing him away. I had to use every ounce of self-control to keep myself sitting there on the ground.

"No." I shook my head and frowned and shrugged my shoulders all at the same time. "I've never heard of it. What's it called again?"

Jimmy Frank's eyes shifted calmly to mine.

His lips moved in a mocking smile.

"See?" Noreen slammed the folder back down, and I casually picked it up and tucked it under my arm. "She doesn't know what you're talking about."

He didn't believe her, of course.

I knew it, and Jimmy Frank *knew* that I knew it.

I caught the last backward glance he threw over his shoulder at me as he and Tyler walked away, and I saw that I hadn't fooled him for a second.

That scared me.

I wasn't sure why, exactly. . . .

But knowing that Jimmy Frank was on to me scared me a thousand times more than any haunted locker.

12

I could hardly wait for school to be over.

When Aunt Celia asked us if we wanted to take in a movie that night, Dobkin said he'd be bored, and I said I had too much homework. It was nice having the house to ourselves. That way we could spread everything out on the kitchen table and not have to worry about what we said. It wasn't that we didn't trust Aunt Celia. It's just that we both agreed she had a lot on her mind right now, with the move and getting settled and all, and there was no use upsetting her till we really knew ourselves what was going on.

"That's her, I'm sure of it," I said again, looking down at the girl's photo in the article.

"Same person?" Dobkin asked. "It's not a very good copy. . . ."

"Good enough." I nodded emphatically. "The face in my mirror was all distorted. And there was blood."

"Blood? How do you know it was blood?"

"I just know."

He nodded. He gazed solemnly at the collection of newspaper articles and then back at me.

"So what happened to Suellen Downing?" he asked.

"Okay." I took a deep breath. "This is what we know so far—what everyone else knows. She went to school that morning. She never came home that afternoon. The last time her parents saw her was in her very own yard. She walked to the road in plain sight, turned around, and waved to her mother, who was watching from the kitchen window. Then she headed off down the road to catch the school bus about half a mile away. We know she was at school that day. When she didn't show up that night, her folks got worried and started calling around to friends' houses. Then they called the police. The search went on for weeks. The whole town turned out to help, plus volunteers came in from all the other towns nearby."

"No clues," Dobkin said grimly, and I shook my head.

"No clues. No leads."

"No ransom calls."

I sighed. "Nothing."

He looked sad. He tilted his head and gazed down at the photograph in front of him.

"She was pretty," he said softly.

"Once, yes," I murmured. "But not in my mirror."

Our eyes met in a long silence. At last Dobkin clasped his hands over his stomach and tucked his chin onto his chest.

"So what are *your* clues?" he asked.

"Oh, Dobkin," I sighed, "this is so stupid. So *weird*. I can't even believe we're doing this. It doesn't even seem real to me."

"Well, your friend Jimmy Fink thinks it's real," Dobkin said wryly.

"Frank," I corrected him. "Jimmy Frank. Yeah, I thought I'd freak out when he said what he did. Why would he bring that up, anyway? Almost like he's— he's—*accusing* me of something *bad!*"

"Maybe he knows something about Suellen Downing," Dobkin said matter-of-factly. "And he doesn't want you using your power to find it."

"It's not a power," I burst out, more sharply than I meant to. He looked back at me like a little troll. "I'm sorry, I didn't mean to snap. I don't like you calling it a power. That upsets me."

"Okay, then, a gift."

"I don't want it."

"Excuse me, but I don't think you have much choice."

"Yes, I do. I can just shut it out. I can just convince myself it's not there—"

"Like you've tried to do ever since Mom and Dad died?"

It got real quiet then. I could hear the wind rattling the kitchen window, and the toe of Dobkin's sneaker squeaking on the floor as he slowly shifted his weight from one foot to the other.

"It wasn't you, you know," he whispered. "They didn't die because of you."

Tears filled my eyes. Dobkin's face swam in front of me, and my voice broke as I tried to talk.

"But—don't you see—I had this *feeling*—and then it came *true!*"

"But you had the feeling because it *was* true. You didn't make it happen." Dobkin's voice went husky, the way it does when he's going to cry and tries not to. "Don't you remember? Don't you remember about that night?"

I didn't want to remember—not now, not for those two long years I'd deliberately shut it out. It was just too painful. One day Dobkin and I had had a mother and a father, and by the next day we were orphans.

"You took Mom's picture into your room that night," Dobkin said quietly. "You'd found it in a drawer where she'd thrown some stuff, and you asked her if you could have it, and she said yes. It was by your bed—"

Yes, it was by my bed. Like it's on the nightstand upstairs right now, still by my bed, by every bed I've ever slept in since that night—

"Don't you see?" Dobkin was almost pleading with me now. "It was Mom's *picture. That* was the connection. That's what made you know when she . . ."

He broke down then. I heard his angry little sobs and the way he tried to hold them back, and I got over to him and held him against me until he was all cried out. The house was very quiet. He made a sort of snuffling sound and moved his head against my shirt, and I knew he was using it to wipe his nose. I decided to try and make a joke.

"You know, Noreen's right about the witch thing—

some other century, and I could've been burned at the stake for having this *gift*."

"Only 'cause people didn't understand," Dobkin said.

His voice was very small, still muffled against me. I slid my fingers under his chin and slowly tilted back his head so I could see his face.

"You can use it for something good." Dobkin looked back at me, that look that always goes straight to my heart and melts it. "Police call in psychics all the time to help them with cases."

"You want me to go to the Edison police?" I teased him.

"I want you to make a difference."

He turned his head away. I reached over and ripped a paper towel off the roll on the counter and held it over his nose.

"Blow," I ordered him.

"Someone misses that girl Suellen," he said.

"Blow," I ordered again.

He did. I went back to my side of the table, and he wiped one hand across his eyes with a defiant pout.

"Okay," I said, thinking back. "So far, there're three things."

"Yeah?" He was being surly now, wishing he hadn't cried.

"First, the awful smell in my locker. Second, when I went with Tyler to his cabin, that spell I had after . . ."

I paused, frowning. *After what?* After I lost my balance or after Tyler pushed me?

"That spell I had after I rolled down the bank," I said slowly. "Third, the face in the mirror."

He gazed at me, waiting for me to go on.

"But you know, I smelled something at the river, too. It was different from the first smell, but it was almost scarier."

Dobkin blinked. "Do you know what it was?"

"I've been trying to think ever since it happened. It's just so hard to describe. . . ." I waved my hands helplessly, wishing I could magically pluck answers from the air. "It's all these images—these sensations—hitting me at once, and it's very hard for me to separate them into individual things. Do you understand?"

He nodded slowly. "I think so."

"I remember the panic, and the fear . . . and . . ." I closed my eyes, trying to recall the exact feelings. I willed myself back down by that river, trying to stand up in the weeds and slime—*thick . . . clinging . . . suffocating wet slippery can't breathe*—

"Earth?" I murmured.

I saw Dobkin watching me, slowly scratching one elbow where he had a red Band-Aid.

"Earth," I said again, but more certain this time. "Yes, that's it. Earth—no—*mud!* I was smelling the mud there by the river and yet . . ." I looked at him in despair, feeling the pieces fading, knowing I was losing them again, but not knowing how to stop it. "And yet it wasn't the river, it was somewhere else—"

"That's okay." Dobkin gave me one of his most wonderful smiles, where he presses his lips together and spreads them from ear to ear without opening his mouth. "You're doing great."

"I'm not." I sighed. "It's gone."

He put both his hands down on the tabletop and leaned over the newspaper articles.

"Okay, this is what we have so far. Fear. A dead girl. And mud."

"Sherlock and Watson we're not," I said ruefully.

But Dobkin wasn't listening to me.

I saw his head snap up and his eyes go wide and fasten onto the kitchen window above the sink. And as I spun around, the deep shadows beyond the glass shifted and disappeared, showing only a thin beam of moonlight tossed restlessly by the night wind.

"What is it?" I asked him, and I watched as he lifted his arm and pointed one shaky finger in the air.

"Marlee," he whispered, "someone's out there."

13

By the time I got the door open, whoever it was had gone. I knew it was a stupid thing to do, but after everything else that had happened that day, I think something in me just snapped. All I wanted to do was get my hands on the Peeping Tom who'd scared my little brother.

"Did you see him?" I asked Dobkin, coming back inside and making sure the door was locked behind me. "Did you get a good look at his face?"

Dobkin's eyes were huge and frightened. He looked just like a little kid.

"No."

"Then how do you know someone was there?" I wasn't trying to be mean, I just wanted him to be sure about what he really saw. "The wind's picking up— maybe you just saw shadows and tree limbs moving and stuff."

But he shook his head stubbornly. "No, he was real."

"Then what did he look like?"

"I didn't see his face. He was just . . . there. And then he was . . . gone."

"Dobkin—"

"What I mean is, I saw his *outline*. His head. Like he'd been watching, and just when I looked over there, he went away. So I saw his shape, but not his face. You know . . . as he was leaving."

I was cold all the way into the pit of my stomach, but I didn't want Dobkin to know how scared I was.

"Well, he's not there now," I said matter-of-factly. "Let's make pizza and put a movie on."

"But what about—" Dobkin began, but I cut him off with a yawn.

"I really can't remember any more tonight, Dobkin, and I'm exhausted. Let's talk about it again tomorrow. Maybe we'll find something else out by then."

He acted disappointed, but I knew he was really relieved. Hardly anything scares Dobkin, but that night he asked me to leave the hall lights on upstairs and downstairs, so Aunt Celia wouldn't trip over anything when she came home. I sat on the very edge of my bed to do my homework so I could hear him in case he needed me, and it took him a long time to finally fall asleep.

I knew he hadn't imagined it.

I knew *I* hadn't imagined that feeling of being watched the night before, either.

Tyler?

I didn't want to believe it—didn't even want to

think it. *And you're only thinking it because he lives next door, and he seems like the most logical solution.* But nothing so far about *any* of this had been logical, so there was no reason to start jumping to conclusions now, I told myself sternly.

There was no way I could write a book report tonight. Throwing my tablet on the floor, I turned off the bedroom light and went over to the window, careful to keep far back from the pane. I could see dark scudding clouds and Tyler's house next door, and the massive oak tree and the window just opposite my own. *Tyler's window?* I wondered.

As if in answer to my question, the light came on over there without warning, illuminating part of a bedroom. I could see rock posters and movie posters slapped up on walls, and shelves with books and magazines and cassettes scattered around. And then, as I continued to stare from the darkness, I saw a silhouette pass in front of the window, and I recognized Tyler at once.

He was slipping out of his black coat.

He was tossing his black cap onto the foot of a bed.

My heart lurched and caught in my throat. *A person in black would blend in perfectly with the night. . . . A person in black would never be seen. . . .*

"Are you crazy?" I muttered to myself. "Get away from the window before someone next door reports you!"

But I knew no one could see me, and I also couldn't move away from the window. I stayed right where I was and watched as Tyler disappeared at one end of the room, then reappeared again munching a doughnut. Then he disappeared at the other end of the room, and I could hear the muffled beat of music. He busied himself at the shelves and turned sideways, and I could see him talking into a telephone. He didn't talk long. After about two minutes he tossed the phone away, and then he ran one hand back through his hair, almost like the conversation had upset him. And then he yanked his sweatshirt off over his head.

If I'd known he was going to start undressing, I wouldn't have stayed there that long—but his shirt was off before I even realized. Nothing else came off after that, but I could feel my cheeks burning just the same—totally shocked at myself, yet not shocked enough to move away from the window. He reached for something on a top shelf, his body stretching out slowly—and he was so beautiful, I thought, so sleek and graceful like an animal. And then he turned around, and I caught my breath, afraid he might look straight through the dark and see me hiding there in the shadows of my room.

He walked over to his windowsill.

He leaned his arms upon it and stared out into the night.

In the room behind him someone appeared, and Tyler jumped, as though he hadn't heard anyone come in.

It was Jimmy Frank.

Their voices raised and they seemed to be arguing, though I couldn't make out a single word.

Then Tyler turned back to the window and slammed it shut and jerked down the shade.

I think I actually stopped breathing then.

When that little square of window light had closed completely up, I let out my breath and sank down in a heap on the floor.

I sat there a long, long time.

I sat there and thought about life . . . and destiny . . .

And Suellen Downing . . .

"You need something else," the voice said suddenly from my doorway, and I screamed and scuttled back into the corner before I realized it was Dobkin.

"What are you doing?" I railed at him. "Trying to give me a heart attack?"

The threat didn't phase him. "I've been thinking," he went on seriously. "To figure out what happened, you'll have to find something else of hers to get feelings from."

"Go back to bed," I told him. "It's late."

"Her house," Dobkin continued, as though I liked talking to the air.

"What?"

"You heard me," he said. "We'll have to go where Suellen used to live."

"But we can't just—"

"Why not? You said no one lives there anymore—it should be easy to get inside."

"I don't even know how to find it. I can't remember all the roads we took last night."

"That shouldn't be so hard. Anyone in town could tell you where to go."

I didn't have any more arguments. Dobkin stood by the door and waited.

"Dobkin . . . we are *right*, aren't we? Thinking Suellen wants me to do this?"

"If she didn't," he said quietly, "would any of this be happening?"

14

All I could do in school the next day was watch the clock. I'd asked Aunt Celia if I could borrow the van, and I'd promised to pick up Dobkin from kindergarten, and we'd told her we were going shopping in town. She'd been easy to fool because she wanted to devote the whole afternoon to her sculpting, so I didn't really feel like we were doing anything wrong.

I also didn't really want anyone to know where Dobkin and I were planning to go.

You can't very well walk into a brand-new town and tell people you're trying to find someone who disappeared, and that you know she's dead because she's been communicating with you. Especially not a place like Edison, where outsiders are already considered mortal enemies.

Then I remembered that Tyler had told me I could borrow his cabin, so the first chance I got, I asked him again how to get there. He didn't look the least bit suspicious—in fact, he looked kind of happy that I was going to take him up on the offer. He even told me where the key was hidden and said I didn't ever have to ask permission to go—just to go whenever I felt like it.

Phase one successful.

I don't know why I felt so nervous about going to Suellen's house. I knew it was deserted, but there's something creepy about poking around where dead people used to live. Out on the main road I passed up my first turnoff, and Dobkin had to yell at me to turn around and go back.

"Calm down," he told me sternly. "It's just a house."

"It's easy for you to be calm," I retorted. "You haven't been afraid to open your locker every day."

"I don't even have a locker."

"I was trying to make a point."

"Did anything happen today?"

I shook my head.

"Well, there you go." He sounded smug. "We must be on the right track."

The van was making weird noises, which made me even more nervous.

"If this thing breaks down, I'll kill it," I muttered. Dobkin ignored me and hung out the window, trying to grab the tops of weeds as we chugged along the country roads.

There were a few times I thought I'd gotten us lost for sure, but finally we rounded a bend in the dirt road and there it was—the ugly old house—set back in its weed-grown clearing. I turned off the engine, and we just sat there for a few minutes, looking at it. Now I could see where most of the roof had caved in. The whole thing was sort of leaning to one side, and everything sagged, and all I could think of was how all the life had really gone out of it.

"Come on," Dobkin said bravely, pushing open his door. "We're not going to learn anything staying here."

"It looks snaky." I shuddered. "I can't go in there."

He turned to me accusingly. "So you'd let a six-year-old child go in there all alone? How do you live with yourself?"

"Okay." I sighed, climbing out. "You win."

There might have been a pathway at one time, but the weeds had long taken over. Stepping carefully and trying to make a lot of noise, we made our way to the front porch, then hesitated outside the door. The screen hung from one rusty hinge. I bent down and tried to peer through a window beside it, but the pane was so thick with grime, I couldn't see a thing.

"Well," Dobkin said. "After you."

"Thanks, you're so considerate."

I resisted the urge to knock. I tried the knob, and after a few determined twists, I felt the door start to creak open.

"Anything yet?" Dobkin hissed at me.

To tell the truth, I was a little surprised myself. After what had happened at the locker, I'd been preparing myself to be bombarded with images and feelings from all sides. But nothing happened. I just felt like a nervous trespasser who wished she were safe at home.

I stepped cautiously across the threshold.

"Anything yet?" Dobkin hissed again.

"Will you be quiet?" I said irritably. "I promise you'll be the second to know."

He nodded and followed me, being careful to step exactly where I stepped. The place was filthy—rain had come in, leaving mold and mildew and rot, and the stench of animal droppings was everywhere. Dobkin took a whiff and promptly held his nose.

"Something died, I think," he said through pinched nostrils.

"What was your first clue?"

It was really rank, and I fanned the air in front of my face, eyes darting back and forth, ready to bolt at a second's notice. There were only a few rooms and no furniture to speak of, but it was clear that people had broken in over the months and left their garbage behind. I couldn't even picture someone living here, much less try and pick up their psychic signals.

Dobkin looked disappointed. "Nothing?" he asked me.

I shook my head. "Let's go. This place is disgusting."

"One more minute. We haven't seen the kitchen yet."

The kitchen turned out to be the most repulsive room of all, and I put my arm around Dobkin's neck to keep him from stepping in. Sewage had backed up into the rusty sink and spilled out across the floor, and flies were thick everywhere, the air vibrating with their buzzing.

"I think I'm going to be sick."

I rummaged in my pocket for a tissue and pressed it against my nose. In the protective circle of my arms, Dobkin pressed into me and buried his face against my stomach.

"Anything yet?" His voice was muffled, and in spite of everything, I had to laugh.

"You don't give up, do you?" I shook him by the shoulders. "You're bound and determined we're not going to leave here empty-handed."

"Empty-minded," he corrected me. He tugged on my hand and forced me to take three steps onto the cracked linoleum. "Come on, Marlee, you must feel *something!*"

"You mean, besides nauseated?"

I started to laugh again, but suddenly my eyes shot like magnets to one corner of the room.

"Ssh—Dobkin—did you hear something?"

He pulled away from me and followed the direction of my stare with his eyes. Shaking his head, he started to say something, but I put a warning finger to my lips.

There was a doorway in that far corner. It opened straight out onto an enclosed porch, where piles of junk were buried in dust and spiderwebs. From where I stood I could also see part of one window out there, its rusty screen twisted in and hanging down one wall.

"What is it?" Dobkin mouthed, but I shook my head and pushed him firmly back behind me.

"Stay here," I mouthed back to him, and once more he nodded.

It was the creepiness of the place, I tried to tell myself as I picked my way carefully across the kitchen floor. It was making me imagine things—hear things —see things moving from the corner of my eye.

For just one split second I thought I'd heard that porch creaking.

For just one split second I thought I'd seen something move beyond that window.

I glanced back at Dobkin. He was standing as straight as could be, his feet planted determinedly, as if ready to rescue me at the first sign of danger.

"Stay there!" I jabbed my finger at him to show I meant business, then I jabbed it toward the window, and then toward the porch. He didn't look so brave then. He glanced back over his shoulder and molded himself flat against the wall.

The porch was an impossible mess of garbage and decay. Weeds grew up through the splintered boards, and small bleached bones littered the floor. There were mouse droppings everywhere. I froze in the middle of the cramped space and strained my ears through the quiet. I could hear my heart pounding and the sound of my own harsh breathing. *You must have imagined it. . . . Nothing could hide out here without making a whole lot of noise. . . .*

I was afraid to get too close to the window. The floor was in such bad shape, I knew it wouldn't hold my weight, and I could hear things scurrying away from me beneath the piles of trash. Shuddering, I took a step back and rubbed goose bumps from my arms.

Why would anyone be out here anyway? This place ought to be condemned.

"People break in sometimes . . . looking for food and a dry place to spend the night . . ."

"Dobkin," I said softly, "let's get out of here."

And suddenly the whole place seemed threatening—a wasted, tragic testament to memories and death and unsolved questions.

"Dobkin?" I murmured.

My eyes went slowly up one of the walls, and I saw where several pipes were showing through the rotting plaster. One pipe seemed darker than the others, and as I watched it, I suddenly saw two tiny points of light gleaming out at me.

"Run, Dobkin!" I shouted. "There's a snake!"

Whirling around, I raced toward the door where I'd left him.

But Dobkin was gone.

15

Dobkin!" I screamed. "Where are you?"

In a mad panic I stumbled back through the house and out onto the front porch, nearly collapsing when I saw him standing by the van.

"What—" I sputtered, "what do you think you're doing, scaring me like that!"

"There was a snake in there," he said calmly. "You know how much I hate snakes."

He looked annoyed with me. I fluctuated between wanting to hug him and wanting to pull his hair out of his head. Instead I summoned every ounce of self-control and marched out to the van and climbed up into the seat.

"You could have warned me," I said sternly.

"I thought you saw it. You practically stepped on its head."

"I did not! It was hanging there in the pipes!"

117

He looked at me blankly. "You mean . . . there was another one?"

"Oh, God . . ." A shiver shook me from head to foot, and I reached across and shoved open his door. "Just get in here and be quiet, will you?"

"Well . . ." He hesitated, summing up the situation. "Are you mad?"

"What do you think?" I muttered. I shoved the key in the ignition, and the van gave a shudder to match my own. "Dobkin"—I sighed—"will you just get in here and close your door so we can leave? *Please?*"

He shrugged and got in, and we took off in a cloud of dust to search for the main road.

"So," he said, looking at me as if I'd flunked an important test, "you didn't feel anything."

"Let's not talk about it, okay?" I said abruptly. I couldn't stop thinking about what had happened back there on the porch—not the snake, but that feeling that someone had been there with us . . . watching . . . listening . . . I didn't want to think about it, but I couldn't seem to shake it.

"The van's acting up again," Dobkin said.

"Let's just pray we get home before it decides to quit," I muttered.

But of course my prayers weren't meant to be answered that day. Why should they—when everything else so far had been going wrong?

We hadn't gone a whole mile before it started sputtering and bucking something awful, and with a huge groan it coasted to the side of the road and died.

"No." I leaned forward and banged my head on the steering wheel. "No! I don't believe this! *No!*"

Dobkin didn't say anything. He opened the glove compartment and rummaged around for a few seconds, then pulled out a very stale-looking candy bar.

"Half?" he asked.

Food was the last thing on my mind, but I took it anyway. I needed something in my hands to keep from destroying the van piece by piece.

"No one will find us out here," I said glumly.

Dobkin stared at me. "Someone will find us."

"No one will ever come."

"Someone will." He pried a cashew from the spotted chocolate and held it up to the light before popping it into his mouth. He chewed slowly.

"We'll have to spend the night out here, and Aunt Celia will be frantic. She won't have the slightest idea where we've gone." In growing despair I let my eyes sweep down the road as far as I could see. The shadows were lengthening, and the birds had gone all muffled.

"Look," Dobkin observed. "Everything's so still. It doesn't even look real."

"I don't suppose in that astute brain of yours you can figure out how to make this thing run?" I asked without much hope.

"Sometimes Aunt Celia sticks it with something."

"Sticks what with what?"

"I don't know. I've never paid that much attention."

I got out then. I got out and lifted up the hood and looked under it without a clue as to what I was looking for. Dobkin got out on the other side, walked slowly around the van, then called to me.

"There's someone coming," he announced.

"What?"

But I could hear it now—the low, uneven rumble of a motor in the distance, growing louder and closer. It sounded so eerie out there with dusk falling around us, and Dobkin and me all alone with a car that wouldn't work, and not a soul around for miles and miles.

"What'll we do?" Dobkin was standing close to me now, and we could hear the engine slowing down . . . slower and slower. Instinctively I looked around for a place to run, but there was just woods, and I wasn't about to go in where I didn't know my way.

It was a pickup truck.

We saw it crest the hill about a quarter mile away, and then come down. It crept along the road, and then it finally pulled off.

The engine stopped.

Dobkin slipped his hand into mine, and we watched as a tall figure climbed out and started toward us through the shadows.

"Trouble?" he asked.

I stared at him. I knew the voice, yet instead of feeling thankful we'd been found, I only felt a strange sense of uneasiness.

"Trouble?" he asked again, and Jimmy Frank stopped a few feet away from Dobkin and me.

He didn't even seem surprised to see us there.

"Hi," I said awkwardly. I glanced at Dobkin, knowing how weird the two us must look, almost as if we'd been waiting for Jimmy Frank to come along. "The van won't start," I added with a glance in that direction. "I don't know what's wrong with it."

"If you have a cellular phone," Dobkin suggested politely, "we could call for a mechanic."

Jimmy Frank made a sound in his throat that might have been a laugh.

"Cellular phone. Right." He walked over to the van and bent low inside the hood. "Let's take a look."

I kept waiting for him to ask why we were out there, but he didn't. I wondered if somehow he knew, and that made me more nervous than ever. It seemed to take him forever to look at the van, but finally he straightened up and pulled a handkerchief from his hip pocket and slowly wiped his hands.

"Looks like someone's been fooling around with your gas tank," he said.

"What do you mean?" I burst out indignantly, and Dobkin gave me a quizzical look.

"I mean there's sugar here on the rim of the cap. No wonder it won't run."

"Sugar? But that's im—"

I broke off, remembering that noise in the house . . . the movement by the window . . .

"What's wrong?" Jimmy Frank was watching me, and somehow I managed to keep my face a perfect blank.

"Nothing. I'm just wondering how we'll get home."

"I won't even be able to push you," he said. "You'll have to ride along with me to town."

I didn't say anything. I bit my lip and looked at his truck and then down at Dobkin.

"It's okay," I said with more confidence than I felt. "I know him."

Dobkin looked like he didn't quite believe me, so I added, "This is Jimmy Frank. I go to school with him."

Jimmy Frank turned around and strode back to his pickup, and I guessed he meant for us to follow. Dobkin looked at me for confirmation, so I put my hands on his shoulders and steered him over to the truck.

"Is there room?" Dobkin asked doubtfully as he squeezed in between Jimmy Frank and me. "I feel like egg salad."

Jimmy Frank threw him a funny look, so I said quickly, "That's his favorite."

"What is?" Jimmy Frank looked like he didn't really want to know.

"Egg salad," I explained. "You know. Sandwiches."

Jimmy Frank slammed his door and turned the key. He pumped the engine. Then he shut it off again and shifted sideways in his seat, angling himself back in the corner and looking straight at me.

"You out sightseeing?" he asked. His voice had that low sound to it again, something between angry and dangerous. I took a deep, silent breath before I answered.

"Are you?" I countered.

"I live here," he said. I thought he sounded kind of smug.

"Where?" I challenged him.

"Just over that next ridge, there's a road that cuts back through the woods and leads over to my place."

He might have been lying—I mean, how would I have known? So I shrugged my shoulders as if it made no difference at all to me where he lived.

"You didn't answer me," he went on. "What were you doing out here?"

"Going—driving—" I stammered, and Dobkin looked Jimmy Frank right in the eye.

"To Tyler's cabin," Dobkin said. "He told her she could use it whenever she wanted. She was taking me there to show me."

Jimmy Frank turned his head away slightly, just enough so I really couldn't make out the expression on his face.

"I see," he said quietly.

"Can we go now?" I asked.

His head moved back. His eyes settled on mine and stared and stared till I thought I'd jump right out of the truck.

"Now?" I asked again, trying to keep my voice steady.

He gave a slow nod. "Sure."

To my relief the pickup started moving. Dobkin scooted even closer to me, and I pressed back into the door. For a long while there was silence except for the rumbling and crashing of the truck hitting potholes in the road. Then at last Jimmy Frank came right out with it.

"Rumors say that locker of yours is acting up."

"Rumors say a lot of things. That's why they're rumors," I retorted.

"What do *you* say?" he asked bluntly.

"I say you shouldn't believe everything you hear." I

hoped I sounded breezy and bored, but I don't think it came out quite that way. The truck went on another mile or so, and I shifted my gaze out my window.

"Why are we going so slow? I'd like to get home sometime tonight if possible."

"I'm not going to ruin my tires just to get you home," he informed me.

But after that he did pick up speed a little, and I started feeling a little less nervous. I just wished we could get home where it was safe. I don't know why I felt the way I did about Jimmy Frank—he hadn't really *done* anything to me, and he *had* stopped to help us out—but everything about him made me uncomfortable.

I glanced over at his hands as he drove. Work hands . . . strong and sun-browned and calloused . . . long fingers gripped tightly around the steering wheel. His denim jacket had seen better days—there was a rip in one elbow and the sleeves were full of old stains.

"Why did you come here?" he asked.

His voice was calm, and yet it startled me. I tried to think of something clever to say, but my mind went blank.

"What are you trying to do, shaking everybody up with this locker crap? Can't you think of any other way to get attention? It won't make you popular, won't help you fit in. Just makes you look stupid."

"What!"

I was so shocked by his accusation, I forgot to be nervous. I stiffened up and glared over at him and felt Dobkin tense against me.

"Are you accusing me of—*what?* Trying to get attention? That's the stupidest thing I've ever heard! How *dare* you accuse me of that! If anything, I should be accusing *you—any* of you—of rigging up my locker to try and scare me half to death! Do you think I *like* feeling sick to my stomach every time I have to get something out of there—do you think I *enjoy* these things happening?"

"Why are you so interested in Suellen anyway?"

"I'm not interested in Suellen," I lied. "Why don't you just stop the truck right this minute and let us get out and walk!"

I put my hand on the door, fully prepared to jump out if I had to.

But I never got the chance.

Goose bumps exploded all over me. My throat closed up and went dry, and a surge of half laughter, half tears flooded through my heart, so the sound I made was more like a sob. I put one hand to my mouth, and tears filled my eyes, and every nerve, every sense was on fire—

"Marlee?" Dobkin grabbed my arm. He looked scared.

"Someone she cared about—" I choked. "Here. *Right here—*"

And Dobkin was pulling back from me, his eyes like saucers, and Jimmy Franks's eyes were narrowed in on me and not on the road—

"She was *here* the day it happened!" I cried. "On this road—in this spot—but—but she never got home—I—I don't know—happiness—trust—she

125

trusted someone—went someplace else? Something —something—I don't know! I can't make it out! Oh, Dobkin—"

"Take it easy," he whispered. "Please, Marlee—"

"Right here on this spot in the road where we are now—with someone she *knew*—"

"What the hell—" Jimmy Frank began, but suddenly his head snapped forward and he let out a gasp. *"Look out!"*

The truck swerved violently, throwing me first against the door and then into Dobkin. I could feel the ground bumping beneath us and branches ripping the sides and belly of the truck as we careened off the road and sliced straight into the woods.

I tried to grab Dobkin—to hold on to him—to shield him from what was coming—

But suddenly there was a bone-jarring crash—the sound of ripping metal and shattering glass—

"Dobkin!" I screamed.

Then there was only silence.

16

Just what are you trying to prove?"

It was Jimmy Frank's voice I heard through the darkness. It was so cold and so calm and so furious that it absolutely terrified me.

"Dobkin?" I whispered.

A hand grabbed my shoulder. There was blood on my lips. I could taste it when I opened my mouth, and I tried to wipe it off on my sleeve.

"Dobkin?" I called again shakily. "Dobkin, are you all right?"

"Damn," Jimmy Frank muttered, and this time I realized his voice was trembling just below the surface of his control. "This can't be happening. . . ."

Beside me Dobkin whispered, "I'm okay, Marlee," and I wanted to burst into tears, but instead I burst out at Jimmy Frank.

"What the *hell* are you trying to do? *Kill* us? You *jerk*—just because you don't want me at your stupid school, and you're so narrow-minded and prejudiced —you—you—"

"You saw her, didn't you?" Jimmy Frank broke in. "I would have run her down if I hadn't swerved."

My voice just stopped. I felt like an ice-cold hand had crept into my chest and was squeezing the life out of my heart.

"What?" I looked at him stupidly, barely even aware of Dobkin's hand patting my arm.

"Suellen," Jimmy Frank murmured. "There. In the road."

I stared out the windshield. We'd hit a tree, and there were cracks running out in all directions, and it was getting so dark outside. I was afraid to turn around and look behind us. I was afraid Suellen Downing might be standing behind us in the gloom, looking like she'd looked in my mirror. . . .

"You must have seen her," Jimmy Frank said again. His voice was as flat as a rock. "You said—"

"In my mind," I answered before I even thought. "I meant . . ." I looked into his eyes and sighed wearily. "I meant . . . I saw her . . . in my mind."

It was quiet for a long time. Nobody moved. When Jimmy Frank spoke at last, he sounded drained. Resigned.

"Your mind," he repeated numbly. "Then you weren't lying. You really are psychic."

"Why would someone lie about that?" Dobkin asked, rubbing his head and looking from Jimmy

Frank to me and back again. "Why would you *want* kids to think you're a weirdo?"

I think Jimmy Frank nodded. It was hard to tell there in the dark interior of the truck. I would have loved to drop the whole subject altogether, but I was still trying to come to grips with what he'd just said.

"She . . . was in the road?" I gulped.

"Yes. Suellen. I mean . . ." He hesitated for a long time. "I mean, I know it couldn't have been Suellen. Not really. But I *thought* . . ."

He leaned his head back, hitting it gently against the back window.

"It *was* Suellen. What are you, some kind of a witch?"

"How do you *know* it was her?" I persisted. "How can you be so sure, when you weren't even willing to believe *me?*"

Jimmy Frank groaned. He sounded even more resigned.

"Because," he said at last. "I've sensed her, too."

I felt like I'd been punched in the stomach. I turned away from him and stared out the window into the darkness, and I could feel beads of sweat popping out on my forehead, but I was chilled through and through. *He's lying . . . he's lying and trying to play some kind of trick on me . . . but why? Why would he do that . . . ?*

"I don't believe you," I murmured.

"I didn't believe you, either. So now we're even."

Dobkin didn't say anything at all. I put my hand on his head and felt something sticky, and suddenly realized he must be bleeding.

"You told me you were okay," I gasped, but he calmly pushed my hand away.

"It's *your* blood," he said. "I think *you* bled on me."

I glanced down, searching for a rag of some kind, but Dobkin felt around on the seat beside him and silently slipped something into my hand.

It felt like a bandanna—Jimmy Frank's, I guessed. I started to ask him if it was okay to use, but he was so intent on talking, that I didn't want to interrupt. I pressed it to my lip, then gave it back to Dobkin.

"I've always had a feeling about this road," Jimmy Frank went on quietly. "Ever since she disappeared. Sometimes it was so strong, I wouldn't even want to drive this way. But I never could put my finger on it, no matter how hard I tried to figure it out. I even thought I was going crazy sometimes, feeling things no one else could feel, sensing things no one else could sense. I'd try to make them go away, but I couldn't. And it's not exactly something you can go to the police with, is it."

It was a statement, not a question. I couldn't believe what I was hearing, and even though I wanted desperately to tell him everything I'd felt and sensed and experienced, I just sat there and held it all in.

"If you tell anyone about this!" Jimmy Frank whirled on me. "I mean *anyone*—"

"No"—I was shaking my head and trying to stay calm—"no, of course not—"

"Damn!" He slammed his fist onto the steering wheel and glared at me. "Of all times to—of all people—"

"I've got to get home," I whispered.

He shifted his gaze to the broken windshield. He bit hard on the inside of one cheek.

"Please," I said.

He shifted the truck in reverse and put his foot on the gas, but the truck just groaned. It sat there smashed up against the tree, and I could hear the motor grinding and the wheels spinning, and after a few minutes Jimmy Frank snapped off the key.

"Nice night for a walk." He sighed, shoving open his door. "Let's do it."

Everything about it was so dreamlike—the three of us climbing out of the truck and starting off down the road. The moonlight filtering down through the clouds in the sky, the road snaking off and disappearing through the trees. I had this eerie feeling that if we followed it, we'd just walk through the shadows and disappear off the face of the earth.

Just like Suellen . . .

My mind was going in a million directions at once. I kept thinking about what Jimmy Frank had said—what he'd admitted to me—but each time I sneaked a look at his face, his expression was so grim, I was afraid to bring anything up again. Maybe he didn't say it at all, I tried to argue with myself. *Maybe I blacked out for a minute in the wreck and just hallucinated everything. . . .*

"Where are we going?" I spoke up as we came to a crossroads. He didn't answer, and when I instinctively turned toward one road, he turned down another.

"Back this way," he said.

"I thought town was this other way—"

"You have a terrible sense of direction, don't you."

He sounded mildly annoyed. "I think I know which direction to go—it's not like I haven't been this way a million times."

I clammed up. The route didn't seem right to me, but I couldn't very well not go with him. Not with Dobkin trailing along behind, trusting both of us to get him home. So I went, but I kept glancing back over my shoulder, thinking we should have gone the other way.

We walked a long time without speaking.

Dobkin kept up bravely, but before long I could tell his feet were starting to drag. I pretended to have something in my shoe and deliberately lagged behind so I could stay in step with him. Jimmy Frank stopped and waited for us to catch up.

"Come on, pal," he said, and before I knew what was happening, he scooped Dobkin up in his arms and started walking again.

"Hey!" I yelled. I thought Dobkin might freak out—number one, he hates being carried, and number two, he's not that keen on strangers. But Dobkin looked back at me over Jimmy Frank's shoulder, and though he looked slightly startled, he didn't seem to mind the ride.

"We've still got a long way to go," Jimmy Frank said, picking up the pace. "And it's too far for this little guy to keep up."

I hurried after them. It was so dark now, I could barely see the road up ahead. Trees rustled around us, whispering secrets, stirring shadows into weird, frightening shapes. I felt like there were invisible eyes watching from everywhere, and suddenly the image of Suellen's watery face popped into my mind, and I gasped out loud.

Jimmy Frank turned around, and I ran up beside him.

"What you said back there," I blurted out, "about Suellen!"

"What about it?" he growled, starting off again.

"You weren't lying, were you? About sensing her?"

"Why would I lie about something like that?" Now he sounded really angry. "Just drop it, will you? I wish I'd never brought it up."

"Well, wh-what I mean is," I stammered, not knowing quite what to say, "is that I want to know what you've . . . you know . . . sensed."

He didn't answer, just kept walking. Dobkin's head drooped down onto his shoulder, but Jimmy Frank didn't seem to notice.

"I know what it's like!" I insisted, trying to keep up with his long stride. "Knowing how crazy you'll sound and being afraid people won't believe you—how things pop right into your mind when you don't want them to, and it makes you so scared . . ."

My voice trembled. I was afraid I might cry, and the last thing I wanted to do was to break down in front of him.

"Jimmy Frank, I've got to know!" Lunging for him, I grabbed his arm and forced him to a stop. He looked down at me, surprised, and I burst out, "I've got to know what you've felt about Suellen!"

He looked down at me for a long time. I couldn't

exactly see his face in the dark, but I could feel his eyes burning into mine.

"Come on," I whispered. "I feel really alone in all this. Please."

He started walking again, but more slowly this time, so it was easier for me to keep up.

"Not knowing what happened to someone," he murmured. "There's nothing quite so awful as that." He was silent a moment, and then his voice grew hard. "Just having someone completely disappear without a trace. Nothing shakes you up like that. Not knowing if they went off somewhere . . . if they're dead . . . what happened."

I started to tell him I knew Suellen was dead, but he went on, so I kept quiet.

"Especially in a place like this—it shook up the whole town. You've got to understand, people here were never afraid before that. They never locked their doors or got scared about their kids or worried about being alone or getting inside before dark. And it made them even more suspicious of strangers."

I thought about this a moment. At last I said, "So what do most people think happened to her?"

"There were a lot of outsiders around then. Because of the highway being built. Lots of drifters . . . guys looking for temporary work. At first everyone was so hopeful she'd be found . . . they just knew a clue would turn up somewhere. But then . . ."

The silence dragged on. From somewhere in the distance a dog howled at the moon.

"People started accepting the fact that she was gone

for good." Jimmy Frank sighed. "I mean, what else *could* they think? They figured some drifter passed through town—got rough with her—hid her where no one would ever find her again."

I shuddered violently. I tried to keep the image of Suellen's face out of my mind.

"But . . ." I pressed him cautiously, "you sensed her. When? Right away?"

Dobkin gave a soft moan. Jimmy Frank shifted him to his other shoulder before he answered.

"No. And it wasn't a constant thing, either. Just every so often I'd get this . . ." He seemed to be groping for words, so I helped him.

"Twinge," I said wryly. "A twinge of feeling—or emotion—or whatever you want to call it. Most of the time when you least expect it. Or want it."

"You understand," was all he said to that.

"Were you close to her?" I asked.

"No closer than anyone else. I went out with her a couple times. A lot of guys did. She hung out with some of the girls, but none of them were what you'd call best friends."

The shadows pressed closer onto the road. I moved closer to Jimmy Frank.

"So what have you sensed about her?" I asked.

"Look," he said, stopping and turning to face me. "I have to live in this town. I have to face these folks every day. They don't like people who're different. They don't understand things like this. I know what I *feel* . . . and I know what I *saw* back there in the road. But if this ever got out—*ever* got out—"

"I swear," I said, and I laid my hand gently on his arm. "I swear to you, I'll never tell a single soul. I know what it's like. I know how you feel. It's something I've tried to hide—to deny, really—for a long time myself."

He sounded suspicious. "What do you mean?"

"My parents died two years ago, and I knew when it happened. They had a car wreck and . . . and . . . I knew."

Another long silence. "I'm sorry," he mumbled. "I didn't know."

"Some people say it's a gift." I sighed. "But I think it can be a curse, too. Feeling other people's pain and fear. If I had my choice, I wouldn't want it. I wouldn't wish it on anyone."

He seemed to mull this over. He started walking again.

"So *you* felt something about the road," he said softly, "just like I have. Funny thing is, sometimes it's as normal as can be. But other times, it's like the air is *charged.* Like some kind of force is there reaching out to you. You *expect* something to happen."

Dobkin made another sleepy sound, and I reached for Jimmy Frank's arm once more.

"He must be getting heavy. Why don't you let me carry him?"

"It's okay. I'm not tired."

"I wasn't telling the truth back there when you found us," I said.

"What do you mean?"

"I wasn't going to Tyler's cabin. I went to Suellen's house to see if I could pick up on anything."

"I figured it might be something like that," he threw back at me.

"But I didn't sense anything. Not till we got to that spot on the road. And then it was so strong! I *know* she was there—with someone familiar that she trusted!"

"And you said it was the day she disappeared?"

"Yes, I'm sure of it."

"And you think this person was . . . tied in some way . . . to her disappearing," he said slowly.

"Yes. I'm sure of that, too." I thought a moment and then looked up at him. "Don't you have any ideas? A friend of hers? Some boyfriend she had? You must have *some* sort of clue!"

"Whoa."

He stopped abruptly. He knelt down in the middle of the road and lowered Dobkin to his lap and gazed down into Dobkin's peaceful face.

"Marlee . . ." he said slowly, "careful now. I don't think you realize what you're saying—"

"I know exactly what I'm saying. She wouldn't have been with this person if she'd been afraid of—hey!" I shouted as Jimmy Frank hoisted Dobkin back onto his shoulder. "Hey, what's wrong? Wait up!"

Jimmy Frank was striding away, like he didn't want me to catch up with him this time, but I ran after him anyway and pulled on his arm until he finally turned around.

"What's wrong with you?" I demanded. "Don't you want to help her?"

"And how could I help her?" He sounded impatient. "Every single theory's already been thought of! Edison and every other town within a hundred miles of here were crawling with cops for weeks and weeks! What could anyone *possibly* come up with that they didn't already think of?"

He shook me off, but I was just as stubborn.

"Come on," I pleaded, "wait a minute!"

"You don't understand how it is here!" he threw back at me, so angry now that his voice was shaking. "People have *forgotten* about Suellen and what happened to her—they *want* to forget! As far as they're concerned, whatever happened to her can't be changed, and she's miles and miles away from here by now—otherwise she would've turned up when they went over this place with a fine-tooth comb! You start stirring things up again and making accusations, and I promise you, it'll cause problems—"

"But I don't think she's miles away at all! I think she's still around here somewhere!"

It popped out before I could stop it, and it shocked me more than it did him, but I still couldn't seem to shut up.

"That's the trouble with this town! They all want to pretend it never happened—they want to believe it was an outsider who did it! But you know what I think? I think it could have been someone right here! I think instead of being so suspicious of *outsiders,* they should start being suspicious of each *other!"*

"Christ," he muttered. "You . . . you think she's still around here somewhere? *Here?* Why did you say that?" He whirled on me, his face cold and furious. He took a step forward, and I backed up.

Suddenly there was the sound of a car coming, and

in the next instant one raced around the curve of the road, pinning us with its headlights.

I felt Jimmy Frank's hand on my shoulder, pulling me out of the way as a car screeched to a stop beside us.

"Hey," Tyler said, leaning out the window of his Mustang. "Need a lift?"

I could see Noreen in the seat beside him, leaning across his shoulder, staring out at us with surprise.

"What's the matter with you two?" Tyler laughed. "You look like you've seen a ghost!"

17

I couldn't stop thinking about what had happened.

After Tyler and Noreen picked us up, I couldn't think about anything else.

We didn't tell them much, really.

I used the story about Dobkin and me going to Tyler's cabin and having the van break down and Jimmy Frank stopping to help. Jimmy Frank told them a deer had run in front of us, and he'd had to swerve to miss it and crashed the truck into a tree.

They seemed to believe us.

It turned out they were going to Tyler's cabin themselves to take some supplies his mom wanted to use there for the summer, and they couldn't get over how lucky they'd been to find us. They asked if we minded going with them first, and of course I had to say no, I didn't mind, even though all I wanted to do was get home so I could sort everything out in my mind and try to make sense of it.

Thank goodness it didn't take long. After we finished at the cabin, Tyler dropped Jimmy Frank off at his house, then went on to town with Noreen and Dobkin and me. Dobkin fell asleep on my lap. Noreen rode in back and leaned forward between the bucket seats. Tyler entertained us the whole way by singing every song that came on the radio.

"Don't worry about your van," he assured me as the lights of town finally came into view. "I'll call the gas station and have a tow truck come out and get it in the morning."

"Thanks, I really appreciate it." I gave him a half-hearted smile and felt Noreen squeeze my arm.

"You're awful quiet tonight," she said. "Something wrong?"

And even though I'd promised myself I wouldn't talk about it anymore, I couldn't help myself.

"Just being out there on that road." I sighed. "It was so spooky. So isolated. You feel so helpless in a situation like that. . . . If anything happened to you, probably no one would ever know the truth about it."

"Stop!" Noreen shuddered. "That sounds like Suellen."

"But I *did* think about Suellen," I said softly. "I can't seem to stop thinking about Suellen. . . ."

Tyler reached over and turned the radio louder.

"Do you ever think about Suellen?" Noreen asked him, but when he only shrugged his shoulders, she glanced quickly at me. "Sometimes I think about Suellen," she murmured.

She lowered her head, and I nodded sympathetically.

"I mean, how can anyone *not* wonder what really happened to her?" Noreen went on. "If she just left town or if she's—"

"Stop it, Noreen," Tyler said quietly. "Just leave it alone."

"But you know what I mean, don't you?" Her voice rose in earnest. "You wonder what her last minutes were like. Was she afraid? Was she happy? Did she know what was happening to her?"

"God, you're morbid." Tyler made a face and squirmed in his seat. "You two are giving me the creeps."

"Well, it *is* creepy," Noreen insisted. "And I thought I'd really gotten over it. I mean, I hadn't been thinking about it at all till Marlee got stuck with Suellen's locker."

Tyler's eyes widened in annoyance. "Will you stop it? If you keep putting ideas in her head, she'll keep imagining things."

"I didn't imagine anything," I said stiffly. "It happened just the way I said it did. Just because *you* didn't see it happen doesn't mean it didn't."

"Touché," Tyler mumbled, a hint of admiration in his voice. Noreen nodded in silent affirmation. I tried not to, but I just had to ask one more question.

"Her parents," I said. "How can they go on, day to day, just wondering?"

"Everyone felt sorry for them." Noreen's voice was tight as she shook her head. "They never gave up hope. They just kept believing she'd turn up, that she was . . ."

Her words trailed off. Tyler finished her thought.

"Safe. Alive somewhere."

"She didn't have brothers or sisters," Noreen mumbled. "She was the only child they had."

For a long moment Tyler stared out the windshield. "They didn't want to move. They really believed she'd come home one day, and they wanted to be there when she did. But the construction job ended, and her dad had to find work."

"I can't imagine," I whispered. "I just can't imagine what that would be like."

"Would you think of your parents at the end?" Noreen went on, talking more to herself now than to us. "Would you be wondering if they were worried about you . . . if they'd already given up hope? Would you be thinking about how warm and safe home is . . . knowing you'd never see them again—"

"Stop!"

Tyler slammed so hard on the brakes that the car skidded. If Noreen hadn't flung out her arm, poor Dobkin would have slid right onto the floor.

"You're making Suellen sound so . . . so . . . sentimental or something!" Tyler's look was incredulous. "You know that *nobody* liked her, Noreen. I mean . . . everyone was sorry it happened, but nobody ever really liked her."

I stared at him in confusion. "But . . . I thought—"

"Well, sure, nobody would ever *wish* something like that on anyone," Tyler said defensively. "But *nobody* liked her. She didn't have any friends. She wasn't popular. The first few weeks with all the publicity and news coverage, everyone was all sorry and stirred up about it. But then things got back to normal. And it wasn't like there was this huge void in school just 'cause Suellen wasn't there. No one paid any attention to her when she *was* there."

I couldn't have been more surprised. I looked at Noreen to see what she had to say about it, but she was staring at the floor.

"Well"—Tyler nudged her impatiently—"am I right or not?"

It took a few minutes, but Noreen finally nodded. "I felt sorry for her," she said, almost reluctantly. "She wasn't very pretty or—"

"Yes, she was," Tyler spoke up. "She was very pretty, let's be honest here."

"Well, your concept of pretty and my concept of pretty are obviously very different," Noreen said indignantly. "And her personality was—well—"

"She didn't have a personality."

Noreen threw Tyler an impatient glance. "She showed off in class, tried to act like she had the answers to everything all the time. And she flirted a lot with guys. Especially the ones who already had girlfriends. Most of the girls didn't like her 'cause of that."

"Most of the guys didn't like her, either," Tyler retorted. "She was weird."

"Understatement, Tyler. She was absolutely, madly in love with *you.*"

Again I stared in surprise. Tyler gave Noreen a reproachful glance and shook his head.

"No, she wasn't."

"Yes, she was, and you know it."

"How can you say that?" Tyler threw back at her. "She was in love with *every* guy. Or at least, she thought she was."

"Hopelessly in love with him." Noreen turned to me, as if Tyler wasn't even there. "Everyone knew it, and Tyler knew it, too. He was just embarrassed 'cause everyone teased him about it."

I looked over at Tyler, who was looking plenty embarrassed now.

"Well, it isn't like I encouraged her," he mumbled.

"No, of course not," Noreen said dryly. "You just looked at her with those big brown eyes, and the poor girl never had a chance."

Tyler recoiled at that. "Don't give me all that 'poor girl' stuff. She was the queen of manipulation."

"And this coming from a guy who can get anything from anybody"—Noreen sighed—"especially if the anybody is a female." She rushed on before Tyler could object again. "Okay, he's right about that," she conceded. "Suellen *was* a manipulator. She wanted to belong, but she didn't. She would have done *anything* to be accepted.

"She made up things," Noreen recalled, her face going grim. "She lied. And tried to come off as special and important and knowing things nobody else knew, just so people would pay attention to her. I guess she thought that meant they were accepting her."

"All they were doing was laughing at her," Tyler said.

"I think she knew they were laughing." Noreen's expression was somewhere between disgust and sadness. "But negative attention was better than none at all, I guess." She got quiet for a minute, then added, "She really had the hots for Tyler, though."

"She did not!" Tyler protested again, his voice rising slightly. "Will you stop saying that?"

"It's the truth. And really, Tyler," Noreen said sternly, "you could have done lots better than Suellen Downing."

"Like it's your business. Who are you, my mother?"

"No, thank God. If I had a son like you, I'd sue the doctor for damages."

Tyler's mouth opened, but Noreen wasn't phased.

"Look," she rushed on, hardly stopping to take a breath, "I never told you this before 'cause you're new, and I didn't want to upset you, but some kids *do* say Suellen's ghost still haunts the school and—"

Tyler groaned. "Noreen!"

"And kids have heard footsteps in the halls after school sometimes, but the halls are empty. They hear doors slamming, and some of them even say they hear ghostly laughter from classrooms, but when they look in, there's nobody there."

"They say those things just to see which kids are stupid enough to believe them." Tyler's voice was patronizing. "And what a surprise! You win, Noreen. You're the stupidest one of all."

Noreen ignored his comment, but turned sideways to look at him. "Maybe Suellen really *is* trying to make contact with Marlee, trying to make everyone realize what really happened to her. Maybe she's been trying to do that all this time, but Marlee's the only one who's ever listened to her!"

Tyler groaned and slid down in his seat.

I thought about all this for a few seconds, then ventured carefully, "If more than one person has sensed Suellen . . . then maybe it's true. Maybe she *is* still there trying to make herself heard."

"Make herself heard?" Tyler sighed again. "She's probably somewhere in another city by now, and if she knew she'd finally caused all this interest in herself, she'd feel successful at last. Not to mention smug."

"Marlee"—Noreen touched my arm and leaned close—"if this stuff *is* true . . . if Suellen *is* trying to make contact with you . . . what do you think she's told you so far?"

I balked. It's one thing to be certain in your own mind about something, but to share it is something else. There's that thing about responsibility. Feeling like I should tell the police, but having no proof. Feeling like I should let Tyler and Noreen in on what I was sure of, but not being able to back it up.

Dobkin nudged me in the stomach, and I said slowly, "It's all mixed up. Sometimes it takes a while to sort it out."

"But you must have opinions," she pressed me. "I mean, I saw your face that first morning when you said something was wrong with your locker. I could tell you weren't faking."

"I think . . ." I began slowly, "I think she felt a

whole lot of fear right before she . . . disappeared. I think she was really terrified. And I think . . ."

Now Dobkin was practically punching me, and I knew Noreen must be able to feel my body jerking with each silent blow. I managed to grab his arms and pin them at his sides.

"What Noreen means is," Tyler said, his glance flicking casually to me and then back to the road, "where *is* Suellen?"

Noreen was staring at me intently. Tyler's hand had started toward the radio dial, but stopped now halfway to the dash.

"I don't know," I mumbled.

"But . . . you think you *could* know, right? That it's possible you'll find out?" Noreen's voice dropped. She was barely whispering, and she wasn't looking at me anymore. "I mean . . . just suppose she *is* dead or something awful like that. You're probably going to know sooner or later, aren't you?"

I glanced at her, but she was staring at the luminous dials on the dashboard. Tyler wasn't looking at either of us, but had his hand still suspended in the air.

"If she *is* dead," Noreen murmured again, "would you know? And . . ."

Her voice faded. She took a deep breath, but it trembled in her throat.

"And . . . would you know how it happened?"

Why was I so afraid to answer? I just sat there squeezing Dobkin tight against my chest, and the air in the car had suddenly gone very hot and very, very close—

"I . . . I'm not sure," I murmured.

"But the truth is, you *could* know," Tyler spoke up at last, his voice steady and reasonable. "The truth is, you *could* know what nobody else has been able to find out. What happened to her. Where she is . . . how she died . . ."

I nodded. "I might," I whispered.

There was a long stretch of silence.

"This is really scaring me," Noreen finally whispered. "I hate things like this—all this weird stuff—"

"I thought you didn't believe in it," Tyler scoffed, and she turned on him, her voice going shrill.

"Well, I never knew anyone like Marlee before—this kind of stuff has never happened around here before! It's really scaring me—of course I don't want to believe in it—I don't know what to think about it!"

"If anyone should be scared," Tyler said solemnly, "it should be you, Marlee."

His warning was so unexpected that I felt a cold stab of fear go through me.

"What? Why do you say that?"

"If I had that kind of gift," he said, and his wide dark eyes shone calmly through the shadows as they settled on my face, "being able to see what others aren't even supposed to know . . . I'd be really scared."

"Of what?" I could feel my throat tightening up, and he seemed to be taking forever to answer—

"The knowledge," he spoke at last. "The connection."

"What connection?"

"Well, if it's true what you've told us, then you and Suellen are connected and she's using you to communicate. So suppose she's dead and you're not . . . what if she just decides to take over? Her mind becoming your mind . . . and you becoming her."

I'd never thought about the possibility before. It was a chilling consideration, and I shivered violently and held Dobkin closer.

"Yeah . . . maybe he's right," Noreen mused, thinking out loud. "And what if you two are so connected, things that happened to Suellen will start happening to you?" She covered her face with her hands and squealed. "I'm scaring myself! Let's not talk about it anymore!"

Tyler made a stab at the radio, and the car filled with music, and he shifted his eyes back to the road once again.

"Maybe it's not such a good thing to have supernatural knowledge," he said quietly. "Maybe there are some things just not meant for people to know."

I was glad when they let Dobkin and me out at our house.

I locked the door tight and stood in the hall a long time, trembling from head to foot, and knowing something horrible was about to happen to me.

18

I didn't get much sleep that night.

I tossed and turned a whole lot and had horrible nightmares. In one of them I dreamed that I went to Dobkin's room and his bed was empty, and I knew he'd been kidnapped, but no matter how hard I tried to picture his whereabouts, I couldn't find him. It was so horrible that I woke up crying, and I gripped the covers to my chin, letting the hot tears roll down my face.

I got up as quietly as I could and tiptoed down the hall to Dobkin's room, and then I stood for a long time beside his bed watching him sleep. He looked so innocent and helpless lying there, with this faint smile on his face and one hand resting against his cheek. I watched him, and I started thinking how ever since Mom and Dad had died, I'd never believed I could ever love anything ever again, but here was Dobkin, my pain-in-the-butt little brother, and the absolute light of my life. And then I reached over and smoothed his hair back from his forehead, and he stirred a little and squinted up at me, all sleepy.

"Marlee?" he mumbled.

"It's nothing. Go back to sleep."

"How come you're in here?"

"Checking your window. It looks like rain," I lied.

That seemed to satisfy him. He was out again in an instant, and I slipped back out into the hall.

Aunt Celia's room was downstairs, and I kept quiet so I wouldn't wake her going back to my bedroom. I'd left the door partway open, and as I approached it, suddenly every hair on my arms stood straight up. I froze in my tracks, one hand raised to touch the door, and something told me not to touch it, not to take one more step across the threshold.

I felt a cold lump of fear lodge in my chest.

I tried to swallow, but there was only cotton in my mouth.

A faint, faint sound floated out through the door. I thought I heard the faint creak of bedsprings . . . the muted thud of something touching wood . . . a muffled tread across the floor . . .

Oh, God . . . there's someone in my room. . . .

My mind spun in a dizzying circle—half of me praying I was imagining things, the other half terrified to go in there. After what seemed like forever, I finally gave the door a little push and froze there in the threshold, a cry lodged in my throat.

Pale moonlight filtered in, angling down through the gnarled tree outside the house, speckling the walls, scattering tiny droplets across the covers of my bed. I could see the curtains flapping crazily in the wind, darkness sucking them in and out my open window, and the empty windowsill, and the huge old branch scraping against it.

It's cruel the way your mind plays tricks on you when you're scared. I stared wondering—did I throw the covers back like that, or had they been moved since I was in there? And when the floor creaked again, I gasped and looked behind me, not sure if the sound had come from inside the room or out in the hallway.

I took a step toward the window.

I didn't leave my closet open . . . did I?

I felt like a little kid—just standing there and staring at that open closet—afraid to go any farther. I opened my mouth to call for Aunt Celia, but nothing came out.

This is silly . . . you're not a child . . . go close the door and get back to bed!

I took a step toward the closet. I heard the soft groan as the door moved slightly, and I jumped back. Shadows seemed to flow from behind the door, to melt right out the window, as though the black, black night had pulled itself from my bedroom. It happened so quick and so smooth that I didn't even have time to blink, and when I finally *did* blink, everything was still as could be.

The closet was still open.

I was still standing there staring into the dark.

I can't believe what a coward you are!

Determinedly I hurried over and shut the closet

door. The corner behind it was empty. I breathed a huge sigh of relief and looked out the window into the swaying branches of the old tree. Leaves gathered and dipped in the wind; shadows squirmed like snakes. Across from me, Tyler's window was a blank square of nothingness. I dived back into bed and burrowed down beneath the covers.

I don't know how long I slept.

It seemed like I'd just drifted off again when something woke me.

I opened my eyes, but I didn't move.

I was lying on the very edge of the mattress and my arm had slipped so that one hand was hanging down off the side of the bed.

My fingers were touching the floor.

I stared out into the darkness, and that's when I heard the sound again—*the sound that had woken me* . . .

It was a slow sliding sound—and in that first confused instant I remember thinking it was like something being pulled along the floor. . . .

"Dobkin," I mumbled, "is that you?"

And it's funny how your mind blanks out just to save you, just to save you from going into shock or dying right there from fright. . . .

"Aunt Celia," I said, "is that—"

And suddenly I realized that my fingers were cold—so icy, icy cold, but the rest of me was so warm, almost hot with all those covers, and I tried to shake my hand, to wiggle my fingers and get the blood flowing again, but they wouldn't move, and so I reached down with my other hand to rub them, thinking they'd gone to sleep—

That's when I realized.

That's when the sudden horrible reality hit me, and I screamed and screamed—

That's when I realized it was someone else's hand coiled around mine upon the floor, and the icy fingers were tightening . . . tightening . . . trying to drag me under the bed.

19

I don't even remember getting to the door.

I just remember screaming and suddenly being out in the hall, and Dobkin stumbling out of his room, and Aunt Celia pounding up the stairs, and everyone trying to grab me and talk all at once. Somewhere in all that chaos Aunt Celia must have managed to disentangle herself and call the police, because the next thing I knew, there were two uniformed men in the hall there with us, trying to calm us down.

"Marlee!" Aunt Celia ordered me. "Marlee, stop it! Tell the police what happened!"

She had me by the shoulders and was shaking me pretty hard, and as I focused in on her face, that's when I realized I must have gone slightly hysterical. Dobkin had his arms around my waist and was holding me so tight I could hardly breathe, and when I tried to take a step, we all three fell in a heap on the floor. It would have been funny if I hadn't been so terrified, but as it was, the policemen helped us all up again and turned on the lights in my bedroom and ushered us back through the door.

"What exactly happened, miss?" the first one asked.

"Tell him, Marlee." Aunt Celia nodded, and she was being stern with me, the same kind of stern she always used when she was trying to get through my panicky state. "Don't leave anything out."

"There's something under my bed," I babbled, pointing, hopping from one bare foot to the other, still feeling the touch of those icy cold fingers pulling on my own.

The second policemen walked slowly over to the bed, and I jumped back and instinctively pulled Dobkin against me.

"No! Don't look under there!"

The man waved his hands at me in a calming motion, and I pressed up against the wall and held my breath. He got down on his knees and tossed up the covers and angled himself downward while he ran his flashlight from one end of the floor to the other.

"Nothing," he said at last, getting back up again, wiping his hands. "Nothing at all under that bed. No offense, miss, but you must have been dreaming."

"It could have been a spider," Dobkin said helpfully. "If a spiderweb wrapped around your hand, you could have thought—"

"They were like ice!" I burst out. "And I think I know what fingers feel like when they're trying to pull me out of my bed!"

I was insulted and angry all at once. I knew how

preposterous this all sounded, but I also knew I wasn't totally off the deep end—not yet, anyway.

"If Marlee says she felt something—" Aunt Celia began indignantly, and the first policeman touched one hand to the brim of his cap.

"A hand in a dream," he suggested kindly. "Dreams can seem pretty real sometimes."

"It *was* real." I held my ground. "Not a dream."

"Then"—thesecondpolicemanscratchedhishead— "where did they go? These fingers of yours?"

I glanced over at the closet and shuddered.

Dobkin retreated to the hallway, shaking his head. "Huh-uh. *I'm* not going to open that closet."

Aunt Celia marched straight over and flung open the door. Of course I knew there'd be nothing there, and I wished she'd stop making such a production out of it.

"Nothing," she declared.

"Why would a person be hiding under your bed?" Dobkin asked.

"He could have come in the window," I pointed out.

This seemed an agreeable solution, and so the two officers both went to the window and stared out at the tree.

"How come you don't have screens on these windows?" one asked, and he gave me a sly wink. "So your boyfriend can sneak in here at night?"

My cheeks flamed furiously. Aunt Celia gave the officers a tight, cold smile.

"They're on order," she said stiffly. "And since the

nights are chilly, and since the furnace in this house gives off heat like the bowels of hell itself, I can hardly expect these children to keep their windows shut and suffocate at night, now, can I?"

The two men exchanged looks. "No, ma'am," the first one said. The second one winked at Aunt Celia, and she looked startled.

"We'll check outside, then," the first one said, throwing me a look that said exactly what he thought of my mental state. "But if it was someone trying to break in, it's most likely your screaming scared him off. He won't be back to bother you, I stake my reputation on it."

I thought of a lot of things I could have said to that, but Aunt Celia, knowing me so well, was shaking her head at me, warning me to keep still. I slammed down the window as she showed the policemen out the front door.

"So?" Dobkin asked from his safe spot near the hall.

"So what?" I muttered.

"So . . . tell me."

"I did tell you. Someone was hiding in here."

"Maybe it was Suellen."

I gave him a scathing look. "Go back to bed."

"I'm serious—maybe she's trying to make contact with—"

"I'm sick of Suellen and her damn problems. Now go back to bed."

He made a face at me and turned away, and then I heard his door slam really hard. I got down on my hands and knees and made my own inspection underneath the bed, and had just sat down on the edge of it again when Aunt Celia came back.

"Come on." She smiled. "I'll tuck you in."

"I'm too old for that," I muttered, and her smile grew sort of sweet and sad.

"Never," she said.

I lay there while she arranged the covers around my chin, and then she sat beside me and took my hand in one of her own.

"You know, your mom would be so proud of you," she said, and we both looked at the picture of the smiling young woman on the nightstand by my bed. "The way you always stand up for what you believe, even when people don't agree."

"Think I'm crazy, you mean," I corrected.

She pursed her lips and thought a minute before she spoke.

"You know, Marlee, I've never liked to pry into your private life. But I have this feeling you're trying to work out some pretty heavy problems right now, and you're feeling really alone."

I glanced at her and barely nodded.

"The other morning when I said you looked strange—well . . ." She took a deep breath and calmly met my eyes. "Your mom used to get that same expression when we were kids . . . when something important was about to happen."

I stared at her for a long while. I don't think it really sank in right away, what she was trying to tell me.

"You're so much like her," she said softly, smiling at the photo and then at me.

"No, I'm not. She was so pretty. I'm so plain."

"Never, darling." Aunt Celia touched me lightly on my hair. "You might not have her face, but you have her gift. Marlee . . . do you understand what I'm trying to tell you?"

I raised up on my elbows and stared at her. "Gift? What—"

"Two days before her accident, she called me and seemed very upset . . . very frightened . . . about something."

Aunt Celia paused for several seconds. Her hand tightened around my own. And when she finally spoke again, I could hear a tremble in her voice.

"She asked me to promise that if anything ever happened to her, that I'd take you and Dobkin and give you a happy life."

"You . . . you never told me that. . . ."

"I was afraid to. After the accident that night, you didn't want anything to do with psychic gifts. You pushed it as far down in your consciousness as it could go. You didn't ever want to deal with it again . . . and I respected your wishes."

I think my mouth dropped open a little. She nodded and let out a deep sigh, and her calm cool hand was stroking mine very gently.

"She had that *same* gift, Marlee, ever since she and I were very small children. She could see things and feel things that none of the rest of us ever could. And she handled it the same way you did—denied it. Ignored it. *Hated* it—because she didn't want to be different. She didn't want the responsibility. Except sometimes she *couldn't* ignore it, you see. Sometimes she couldn't, because the very things she was trying so hard to ignore were much, much bigger than her own will. And then, they just *had* to come through her. She had to *let* them—do you understand—in spite of her own personal feelings. She *had* to, because they were just too important."

I kept staring at her, and tears brimmed in my eyes, and she leaned over and kissed me lightly on my cheek.

"Good night, darling," she whispered.

I watched her disappear into the hallway.

I heard her voice soft, soft from the darkness of the hall.

"Shall I leave the light on?" she asked me.

"Yes," I answered back. "Please."

I lay there and watched the light for a long time.

And then I put my mother's picture beneath my pillow, and at last I slept.

20

"Tyler's having a party Saturday night," Noreen said as we hurried down the hall to homeroom. "You've got to come."

"I do?" I groaned. "Oh, Noreen, I can't—"

"No excuses!" she tried to look stern, but her face crinkled up into a smile.

"But I really have to help Aunt Celia—"

"You can help her on Sunday. Saturday night is party night!"

"So where is this party?" I asked reluctantly.

"At Tyler's cabin." She grinned. "A wish-it-was-summer party. There'll be tons of food and we'll cook out and take music and videos and all sorts of stuff. You've got to come, Marlee—I already said you would!"

"You did?" I couldn't help laughing. "Since when are you my social secretary?"

"Since all the kids are dying to know you!" She giggled. "I mean, it's just not the same as seeing them in school! I've been telling them how much you've traveled around the country, and everyone wants to talk to you!"

I groaned. "Thanks a lot. I won't know what to say to any of them, and it's all your fault if I make a complete fool of myself."

"Too late!" A voice spoke at our backs, and Tyler swung lithely into step beside us. "After the first time you saw ghosts in your locker, your reputation was shot."

Inwardly I groaned even louder. *My wonderful power—the bane of my existence.* It was the very thing I'd tried so hard to avoid, and now it was my one claim to fame.

"They're just curious, that's all," Noreen said, trying to soothe me.

"Like people at the county fair who always want to see the six-legged goat," Tyler deadpanned, and Noreen whacked him over the head with her books.

"Don't you have something else to do besides annoy us?" she demanded, then turned back to me without waiting for his answer. "Okay?" she persisted. "Okay? You'll come?"

She was pinching my arm, and I finally let out a yelp.

"If it's between that or being tortured, I guess I'll choose the party." I gave in grudgingly, rubbing my arm where a little welt was already forming.

"She's merciless," Tyler deadpanned. "Definitely a good person to have on your side."

"I'm so excited." Noreen giggled. "I love parties!"

"You *are* a party," Tyler said. "And *speaking* of parties, am I expected to go down there and clean up the whole place by myself?"

"Of course not." Noreen poked me in the ribs. "We wouldn't *think* of asking you to get ready for your own party, would we?"

"Jimmy Frank's bringing over the coolers tomorrow night so we can go ahead and start icing down drinks," Tyler said.

"What about food? Can we start fixing something ahead of time?" Noreen asked.

He shrugged as if he hadn't thought much about it.

"Men!" Noreen sighed. "It's amazing how they just expect things to happen automatically. Like the barbecue fairy will magically have the burgers there on time . . . and the dance fairy will just wave a wand and presto!—all the right music!"

"We could take care of the food, couldn't we?" I offered. "And I'd be able to come over tomorrow night and help clean."

"Me, too!" Noreen nodded. "Between the four of us"—she tried to look stern—"and I *do* mean the *four* of us, which means you *and* Jimmy Frank have to do your share—it shouldn't take us long to get the place in shape."

I stopped dead in my tracks and stared at her.

"No, I can't come tomorrow." I sighed, and her face crumpled.

"Why not?" she wailed.

"I just remembered—Aunt Celia's going into Freeburg to try and sell some of her sculpture, and she won't get back till really late, and I have to stay with Dobkin."

"So? Bring him along," Noreen said without hesitation, looking over at Tyler, who nodded.

"Sure. He's a cool kid."

"Well . . . I don't know. . . ."

"If you don't come willingly," Noreen said, leading the way into homeroom, "we'll kidnap you."

Tyler looked as though the idea appealed to him, and I knew I'd lost the battle. I could only guess what Dobkin would say about it—he hated being babysat, and he hated cleaning even more.

The day went by quickly, but everything was pretty much a blur to me. So much had happened the last few days, my mind felt numb, and I wished I could just turn it off. Every time I changed classes, I looked for Jimmy Frank, but he never seemed to be around, and I wondered if he'd even come to school today. I wanted so much to talk to him about his experiences —the things he'd sensed about Suellen since her disappearance. I had this terrible feeling he regretted having told me about it, and that it would be a cold day in hell if I could ever get anything out of him again.

"Have you seen Jimmy Frank?" I asked Noreen at lunch, and she gave me a suspicious look above her mouthful of sandwich.

"No. Why?"

"I . . . just wanted to thank him for stopping to help us last night," I thought quickly.

"Forget it." The idea seemed to amuse her. "He

wouldn't want you to make a big deal about it. Aren't you eating?"

"I'm not very hungry."

"We could walk over to the bleachers. He and Tyler might be hanging around there watching the girls run track." She rolled her eyes to show what she thought about this pasttime, and I followed her off behind the cafeteria. We hadn't gone very far when she suddenly looked over at me and said, "He likes you, you know."

I must have looked so shocked, because she giggled and linked her arm through mine and gave me one of her hugs.

"He does, you know," she said again, and all I could do was stammer.

"What—what are you talking about?"

"Tyler, of course. Who else would I be talking about?"

"Noreen, you really are crazy. The rumors are definitely true about you," I shot back, but it didn't phase her.

"I've known him forever, and I can tell these things," she said sagely. "So what do you want to know about him?"

"What do you mean, what do I—"

"It drives him crazy when girls know things about him. So what do you want to know?"

I remembered our drive out to his cabin that night, and how self-conscious he'd gotten when I'd teased him. I smiled to myself, but Noreen caught it.

"Ah-hah! You know what I'm talking about! So how do you feel about *him?*"

"Noreen—" I gave a huge sigh, trying very hard to be patient with her nonsense. "I've only just met Tyler. I haven't even been here a whole week. *You* have the wildest imagination of anyone I've ever known."

"I know." She grinned. "But usually I'm right about things when it comes to Tyler. And I'm right about this, too—you'll see."

We walked on without talking. Several minutes went by, and then finally Noreen glanced over at me, a look that was almost pained.

"I love him, you know."

She wasn't joking now, I could tell. She wasn't smiling anymore, and she was very serious.

"I know," I said.

"Not romantically, you understand," she said quickly . . . too quickly, I thought to myself. "Tyler would never see me that way. We've grown up together. We've been buddies for too long."

I nodded. I saw the way she looked down at her shoes scuffing through the dirt, and I saw the way the corners of her mouth moved in an uncertain frown.

"Anyway, here's the thing. Tyler's going to get away from this stupid town." She squared her shoulders and lifted her chin, almost defiantly. "Yeah!" She smiled. "Tyler's going to get away from here and do *great* things!"

"I believe that," I said sincerely.

"He's going to get a scholarship, did you know?" Noreen went on proudly. "All the teachers are rooting for him—he's got so much support around here. He's going to get it." She nodded again, her voice adamant. "He's *got* to get it."

She ducked her head again and quickened her pace. She raked one hand through her hair and gave it a brisk fluff with her fingertips.

"And what about you?" I asked quietly. "What are you going to do when you graduate?"

"Oh, you know"—she laughed, kicking at a rock in her path—"stay here. Open a beauty shop." She saw my look of disbelief and shook my arm again, more roughly this time. "No kidding—I *love* to do hair! I mean, look at this—" She ruffled her own curls. "Absolutely nothing to work with—all frizz. So I have to get vicarious pleasure from doing other people. I mean, we're not talking just your friendly neighborhood old-lady perms here—I'm talking *big time!* Tanning salons . . . makeovers . . . fake nails . . . even massages!"

"I'll come." I grinned at her. "I could sure use a complete overhaul."

"Unless Jimmy Frank asks me to marry him," she added, casting me a glance that was both wistful and mischievous. "And then I'll move out to his farm, have ten kids, and milk cows."

We stared at each other and burst out laughing.

"Ten kids!" I exclaimed, and she leaned toward me conspiratorially.

"You have to understand the process that entails." She tried to keep a straight face. "It's a nightly ritual that requires complete and selfless dedication."

Again we laughed uncontrollably, not stopping till we reached the athletic field. Noreen spotted the boys at once, perched on the bottom row of bleachers and having an intense conversation, by the looks of it.

They broke off as we walked up, and I thought both of them looked kind of uneasy. I had this feeling we'd interrupted something important, but of course I was feeling so paranoid by that time, I knew I shouldn't trust any of my feelings.

Still hanging on to me, Noreen stopped right in front of Tyler and gave him a sly smile.

"Look who I brought," she cooed, and Tyler's face flushed, though he was trying very hard to look like he hadn't heard her. I could have died.

"Is that your head, Noreen?" he asked casually. "Or is the moon out early?"

Beside him Jimmy Frank stood up and started walking back to the main building. After a brief shoving match, Tyler and Noreen followed, and I trailed after them. We hadn't gone far when Jimmy Frank started to lag behind and eventually fell into step beside me, but the others didn't seem to notice and kept on.

"Thanks again for helping us," I offered, but he didn't really seem in the mood for conversation. His face was grim, and there were hard white lines around his mouth.

"Did you take anything out of my truck yesterday?" he asked abruptly.

I stared at him in surprise. "Like what?"

"Just tell me—you either did or you didn't."

"Hey, I'm not in the habit of stealing things, okay?" I snapped. I couldn't believe his attitude—not when we'd found such common and important ground yesterday, and I'd actually begun hoping he could help me figure things out about Suellen.

He looked like he was going to snap back at me, but then thought better of it. Without a word he strode off and disappeared into the building, leaving me to stare after him with a sick feeling in my stomach.

I didn't understand what was going on.

I didn't understand anything anymore.

I was so glad when class ended that day. Jimmy Frank's accusation had left me in a surly mood, and I didn't even feel like talking to Noreen about it, so I wasted time in the girls' bathroom till I was pretty sure school had cleared out. There was that unnatural kind of hush in the corridor as I walked to my locker. From somewhere upstairs I could hear the low murmur of teachers' voices as they drifted out of empty rooms, and then their muffled footsteps coming down and going out the front door of the building.

I stopped and looked nervously behind me.

Empty.

Just a long stretch of deserted hall.

I quickened my pace and hurried on to my locker. I shifted my books to one arm and nervously fiddled with the lock. I yanked at the door, and it came open easily in my hand.

At first I thought I was seeing things.

I stood there, eyes riveted on the inside of my locker, and everything was *moving*—sides—top—bottom—*everything*—breathing and bubbling and squirming, as if the whole locker had suddenly come alive.

And then it began to melt.

Little pieces coming apart like scabs falling, flaking, flowing right out the door—

Right onto me . . .

And yet I knew better.

I knew even though I couldn't make myself believe it—I knew even as the dark brown pieces of my locker broke apart and spattered out onto the floor and streamed over my shoes and my hands and up the sleeves of my sweater and into my hair—

I didn't even feel them.

I was someplace else now.

Someplace dark and secret where I couldn't move, couldn't see, couldn't call for help, just me and the roaches swarming over me, the maggots gnawing my eyes, the worms crawling out of my mouth— someplace dark and small and silent and not so very far away, and I was there, and I wasn't alive, and I wasn't even me . . .

I was Suellen.

21

Y ou have a fever," Aunt Celia said, laying one hand on my forehead, using the other to hold a thermometer up to the light. "Not much of one, but still . . ."

"I'm just tired," I whispered. "I'm sure it's nothing."

"You forgot to pick Dobkin up after school," she said patiently. "You were walking in the opposite direction when I drove by. You didn't even notice I got the van fixed."

"Tired," I mumbled again. "If I could just sleep . . ."

I saw her concerned expression . . . felt the soft, steady coolness of her hands upon my face.

"Tyler asked about you," she said with forced cheerfulness. "He saw you when we got home, but you weren't in the mood to talk to him. He said to tell you hi."

I closed my eyes. I lay very still.

"Let me help you, Marlee." Aunt Celia smiled sadly, but I shook my head and turned over and buried my head in the pillow. There was a long moment of uncertain silence. I thought she might stay after all, but finally I heard the door close and her slow footsteps fading down the stairs.

Roaches . . . hundreds of roaches crawling all over me . . .

"They were real," I whispered to myself, "weren't they?"

I *thought* they'd been real—they'd *seemed* real as I'd stood there in the hallway and felt them scurrying over my arms and up my neck—as I'd heard them pattering down onto the floor—as they'd raced into cracks and crevices to hide themselves in the dark hollows of the old brick walls. . . .

But they wouldn't be there tomorrow.

With grim certainty I knew that by tomorrow there'd be no trace of them, and even if I told someone, nobody would ever believe me because there'd be no proof it had ever happened. . . .

So maybe it wasn't real after all.

Maybe I imagined it—dreamed it—saw it in my mind just like I saw Suellen's face and smelled her fear and felt her death and aloneness . . .

I slept a deep and dreamless sleep.

I slept without thinking, without feeling, black and empty and merciful.

The room was filled with night when I finally woke up. There was no moon. No starlight sprinkled the sky beyond the windowpane, and a damp, chilly breeze filled the room with dread.

"Aunt Celia?" I whispered.

For just a moment I thought I'd heard something at the window. For just a moment I thought I'd seen a shadow crouched there beyond the sill. . . .

The house was very quiet.

My eyes sought out the clock on my bedside table, and I was shocked to see that it was just after twelve.

There it is again. . . .

I bolted upright, my heart pounding, the sick taste of fear in my mouth.

Something outside my window . . .

Slowly I pushed back the covers and got out of bed. I took one step, cringing at the coldness of the floor on my bare feet. My nightgown billowed out around my ankles, and I clutched it close to my body, trying to stay warm. I tried to call out, but my voice had gone. Trembling violently, I forced myself to walk several more steps until I had a clear view of the window and the darkness beyond it and the massive old tree clawing at the glass.

There's no one out there. I'm going to prove it to myself once and for all—I can't go on being afraid of my own shadow every time I turn around. . . .

I crossed the last few feet and took hold of the window. I felt weak and unsteady, but I shoved till I got it open. For several seconds I leaned out upon the sill, taking deep gulps of cold night air, waiting for my dizziness to pass, and right then and there I made up my mind to ask Aunt Celia to move.

I'll do it tomorrow. Before I even go to school. She'll know I have a good reason for it. . . . She'll have us out of here by the weekend, and I'll never have to hear of Edison or Suellen Downing again.

Having come to a decision about it, I felt like a huge weight had been lifted from my shoulders. I straightened up and felt the chill melt from my bones, a quick surge of heat replacing it. I leaned out farther from my window and lifted my hair up off my neck, and then I closed my eyes and turned my face into the cool, cool breeze.

I stayed that way for a long time.

I stayed there, and I let the tears come, and it didn't matter that I was crying, because there was only the darkness and the deep, deep quiet and no one to hear but me.

At last I lowered my head and gave a final sob.

Then I stared out through the tangled limbs and into the soft, silent shadows.

I never expected to see the eyes staring back at me.

I never expected to see them there only a few feet away, or the branches pulling slowly apart around them, or the long silhouette uncoiling itself from the rest of the tree—

My mouth opened in a scream, but before I could get it out, a hand clamped down over my lips.

"Shhh . . . do you want to wake the dead?"

"Tyler!" I screamed anyway, muffled as it was, behind his fingers. "Tyler, what are you *doing!*"

"If I take my hand away, you have to promise you won't make any noise," he said patiently against my ear. "Promise?"

"What are you doing?" I demanded again.

There was a long, hesitant silence.

Then, "Watching you," he said softly.

I stiffened in his grasp and tried to twist free, but he was too strong.

"It's not what you think," he insisted. "I was worried about you, that's all. Now will you promise to be quiet so I can let you go?"

This time I nodded. I felt the pressure ease on my mouth, and his hand slid away.

"Tyler—" I began furiously, but he held his finger to his lips to shush me.

"You'll stir up the whole neighborhood," he warned. "You've got to be still."

"What are you doing hiding up here in this tree!"

"What are you doing *crying* up here in this tree?" he countered.

I got quiet then. He was looking at me so intently that I finally had to drop my eyes.

"Come on," he said, reaching out to me.

"What? Where are we going?"

"Never mind, just come on. It's okay—I won't let you fall."

I saw his arms reaching out to me . . . I saw the encouraging nod of his head. After a long moment I held out my own arms and felt him gather me up against him and lift me out over the windowsill.

"Tyler—"

"Shhh . . . don't be afraid. . . ."

"What if we fall—we're up so high!"

"We're not going to fall—I come up here all the time."

"But, Tyler—"

"Don't worry, Marlee, you're safe with me."

I put my head against his shoulder so I wouldn't have to see the ground far below. He kept his arms tight around me, maneuvering almost effortlessly through the branches. I knew we were moving farther and farther out on one particular limb away from the house, and when Tyler finally stopped and lowered me down, I realized I was cradled in the protective circle of his arms.

"Tyler," I tried again, but he sighed and gave me a gentle shaking.

"Trees help you think," he said matter-of-factly. "They're good for the soul."

"I can't believe I'm doing this."

"Stick with me, and there'll be lots of things you won't believe."

Once more I felt his lips move upon my ear, and I tried to suppress the shiver that coursed through every vein in my body.

"Cold?" Tyler asked and held me tighter against him.

"Why are you doing this?" I mumbled.

"Why not?"

"What if someone sees us up here?"

"No sensible person would be up at this hour spying on trees. Will you relax?"

Again his arms tightened around me. I could feel the warmth of his skin, and the calm beating of his heart through his shirt. I could feel his hair soft against my cheek, and the touch of his chin as he rested it lightly on top of my head.

"Tell me why you were crying," he said quietly.

I didn't answer right away. A thousand emotions shot through me, all too painful to go into.

"Tell me," he said again.

"I guess . . . because I was tired."

"And *I* guess . . . that's not really the reason."

There was a smile in his voice, and his lips vibrated softly against my ear.

"Do I have to do something drastic to get you to talk to me?" he murmured.

I felt his head lower. I felt his mouth barely nuzzle against my shoulder.

"You *are* cold," he scolded gently. "You're shaking like a leaf."

And I didn't mean to say it, but it came out before I even realized. "I'm so scared," I whispered.

"Of me?"

I couldn't answer. I didn't know.

"Of me?" he asked again.

He tilted my face back. His lips brushed my forehead, my eyelids, the tip of my nose. I caught my breath in surprise, and he was kissing my cheeks now, my ears, and as my pulse raced out of control, his lips covered my mouth, gentle yet demanding. His fingers smoothed my hair back from my face and traced down each side of my neck, and as I trembled violently beneath their touch, they slid slowly down my arms . . . and up again to my shoulders . . . then down once more, finally slipping around my waist, where they stayed.

Pressed against him, I moved my head upon his chest and felt his cheek touch mine. His breath was soft and calm beside my ear, but his heartbeat had quickened to match my own.

"Marlee . . ." he whispered, "what is it?"

And I didn't want to cry—told myself I wouldn't—but his touch was so tender and his voice was so kind . . .

"It's Suellen," I choked. "No matter how hard I try to shut her out, she won't go away. I keep finding out things about her that I don't want to know."

A cold breeze swayed the branches above our heads. Tyler's hold around me tightened.

"What kinds of things?" he finally asked.

And every instinct was warning me not to say anything, not to tell him what I'd discovered—*he'll think you're so weird*—*he'll never want to be with you ever again*—but I felt so warm, so safe inside his embrace—safe like I hadn't felt in such a long time. . . .

"I know Suellen's dead," I said quietly.

I waited for him to say something, but he didn't. As the minutes dragged by, a muscle clenched slowly in his cheek, and the line of his jaw went rock hard.

"Tyler?" I whispered.

"How do you know she's dead?" He seemed to have trouble getting the words out, and I reached up to touch his face.

"I can't really explain it to you. It's just that I see things . . . feel things. They happen, and I can't stop them."

"But you're . . . sure . . . about Suellen? You're sure she's really dead?"

"Yes," I said sadly. "I'm sure she's dead, and I'm

pretty sure her body's hidden somewhere close to here."

He gave a start, as if the corpse of Suellen Downing might suddenly materialize out of the darkness.

"Where?" he asked sharply, but I shook my head.

"I don't know, exactly. But near here—near this town. Somewhere."

"Have you . . . told anyone?" he murmured. "The police?"

Again I shook my head. "Who would believe me? I know how all this sounds—I can't even expect *you* to believe me. I don't have any kind of proof—who's going to listen?"

He seemed upset. I could feel the tenseness of his muscles as his hands locked around my waist. Turning my head a little, I could see his wide dark eyes fastened on the night sky above us.

"What's it like, Marlee?" His voice was low, his lips barely moving as he spoke. "When you get those feelings? When you know all those things?"

So I tried to tell him, tried to explain to him how it was, what happened, how I felt. I didn't expect him to understand, really. It just felt so good to let it all out, to feel warm and safe for a change.

When I finished, he wasn't looking up at the sky anymore. He was looking down at me, and his eyes shone softly and steadily through the shadows. I could tell they were focused full on my face, and their calm intensity made little shivers go up my arms.

"Have you told anyone else about this?" he asked.

"Only Jimmy Frank."

I knew I shouldn't have said it, because I'd promised not to, but it slipped out before I could stop it. Tyler kept quiet, but I could feel his muscles tightening, one by one, and his whole body going rigid. He let go of my waist, and his hands clamped down hard on my shoulders.

"You . . . told Jimmy Frank?" he sounded slightly dazed. "Why?"

"Oh, no." I groaned. I covered my face with both hands and made a sound of disgust in my throat. "Oh, Tyler, I can't believe I just said that, after I swore I wouldn't."

"Wouldn't what? What are you talking about?"

I felt so guilty I could hardly bear to look at him, but he pried my hands away from my eyes and stared at me so intently, that I didn't have much of a choice but to explain.

"Please don't tell him about this." I sighed, thoroughly angry with myself. "He'd be so embarrassed if he thought you knew—"

"Don't worry," Tyler murmured. "Your secret's safe with me."

I nodded, relieved, and tried not to leave anything out. I told him about going to Suellen's house, and the van breaking down, and Jimmy Frank finding us on the road, and the feeling I'd gotten about Suellen being with someone she knew on the day of her disappearance.

"Then Jimmy Frank told me *he'd* been sensing Suellen ever since she disappeared," I said earnestly. "And then, when we were in his truck, he saw Suellen's ghost in the road, and that's when he swerved into a tree."

"Why did he see her in the road?" Tyler asked.

"He thinks because I was with him."

"And what do you think?"

"I . . . I don't know." I shook my head miserably. "I don't know what to think about anything. All I know is that I wish all of this were over with!"

"Is it possible," Tyler went on slowly, "that you and Suellen are tied that closely together? That you're starting to pick up more and more information about what happened to her? That you could actually solve what no one else has been able to?"

Again I shook my head. "I don't know," I whispered.

His arms slipped around me. He drew me close against his chest, and his lips brushed my ear.

"Do you think," he said very softly, "that you could find Suellen on your own?"

I didn't answer. I felt hot and cold all at once, and I couldn't tell if it was from Suellen or from Tyler or from my own exhaustion.

"If I went with you to help?" Tyler added.

His voice was low and persuasive. I closed my eyes, and the night spun in a dizzying whirl.

"I can't just make it come," I said shakily. "It comes when it wants to, and there's never any warning—"

"But do you *think* you could?" He held me tighter. His fingertips traced along my spine, and I gasped in confusion. "Do you think," Tyler persisted gently, "that you could find her if you tried?"

"I . . . I might."

This time he pulled slowly back from me. His eyes

settled on my face, and after a moment he gave me a wink.

"Come on. Let's get you inside."

"But I'm so scared, Tyler," I protested as he helped me back along the tree to the window. "You don't understand—I know I should help for her family's sake, but I don't want to. I just want her to leave me alone."

"But she's not going to, is she," Tyler said matter-of-factly. "Not till you find her. Not till everyone knows the truth. And only you can do that."

I sighed. "I want it to be over."

And he stopped and looked down at me, and there was this faint little smile on his face, but no smile at all in the soft depths of his eyes. . . .

"It will be," he promised. "Soon."

22

hy do I have to clean?" Dobkin asked irritably. "It's not my party. I haven't even been invited."

"You don't have to clean. You just have to come with me because I can't leave you here by yourself."

"You could if you wanted to."

"Well, I don't want to. And stop being difficult."

I glanced over my shoulder at him, then sighed and repositioned myself at the living-room window. *Friday afternoon at last . . . no locker to face for two whole days.*

Of course the roaches hadn't been there this morning, just like I'd known they wouldn't be. I'd spent all day in a fog, wondering if they'd been real or if I'd only imagined them.

I didn't know which was worse.

"I'm sick," Dobkin complained, startling me out of

my worries. Again I turned around to see him frowning behind me.

"You're not sick. And what have you got in your hand?"

"A rag," he mumbled.

"Doesn't look like a rag. Looks like a bandanna or something." I narrowed my eyes at him and sighed. "Did you take that from Jimmy Frank's truck the other night?"

"You were bleeding on me. I was going to give it back."

"Well, take it with you. He's probably been wondering where it is."

"Just a stupid old rag," Dobkin muttered.

"Go on, Dobkin. I'm trying to think."

I turned my back on him and covered my face with my hands. If Suellen *had* sent the roaches, then how many more horrible things was my mind going to subject me to before this whole thing was over?

And if it wasn't Suellen after all . . . if the roaches were real . . .

I could hardly stand to think about that possibility.

I knew if the roaches were real, it could only mean one thing. Someone had deliberately put them there to scare me away.

Someone who knows more about Suellen Downing than they want me to find out. . . .

"Aunt Celia wouldn't like it if she knew you were up in a tree half the night with that guy next door," Dobkin said suddenly, coming up behind me.

I nearly jumped out of my skin. I turned and glared at him.

"I wasn't up there half the night. And we were having a serious discussion, nothing else. And what were you doing out of bed spying on me, anyway?"

"I'll make a deal with you," he said smoothly. "I stay here this evening, and Aunt Celia never finds out about that guy who hangs around in trees."

"Nice try. Get your jacket."

I could hear Dobkin muttering as he slammed the door to his room, and I was just about to tell him it wouldn't do any good to lock himself in when I saw a gray car turn into our driveway. At first I thought it was Tyler, but then Noreen honked and waved out the driver's window.

"Come on!" I yelled at Dobkin. "Noreen's here!"

He didn't answer. He pretended like he hadn't heard and made me come all the way up to his room. I ordered him downstairs, and he sulked a little, but when we got outside, Noreen suggested stopping for ice cream, so he perked up and was even halfway civil by the time we headed out of town and he was nose-deep in a chocolate cone.

"I started a grocery list," Noreen informed me as she turned off the main highway. "I thought we could shop in the morning and just take everything on to the cabin to get it ready. What do you think—pizza or burgers or both?"

"If you have burgers, someone's bound to want hot dogs," I said.

"You're right. But there's always someone too health-conscious to eat hot dogs *or* burgers."

"Vegetarian pizza?" I suggested, and she nodded, as

if I'd stumbled upon some miraculous cure for hunger.

"Perfect. Sodas . . . chips and dips . . . relishes . . . paper plates—plenty of napkins—"

"Dessert?"

"Ice cream." She sighed, and Dobkin finally spoke up from the back seat.

"What if it rains?"

"There's an optimist for you." Noreen made a face into the rearview mirror. "If it rains, we use the microwave, how's that?"

Dobkin lapsed into silence. I could tell he wasn't going to be a bit cooperative about anything, and I mentally steeled myself for an evening of sister torture.

"Your car looks just like Tyler's," I said, glancing around at the upholstery, and to my surprise Noreen laughed.

"That's 'cause it *is* Tyler's. Or at least, it's Tyler's when he's trying to figure out what's wrong with it."

I must have looked confused, because she added, "He's been driving it for the last two weeks 'cause it's got a funny noise and I wanted him to fix it."

I stared at her a minute, something nagging in my mind. At last I said, "So he's a good mechanic?"

"The best. He could take a car apart and put it back together in his sleep."

I glanced at Dobkin in the rearview mirror, but he was staring out his window. For just a second I'd had a flashback to the two of us stranded out on that country road, and Jimmy Frank looking in under the hood of our van and saying that someone had messed with it.

"He should look at our van, then," Dobkin said absentmindedly. "It's always breaking down. Maybe he could fix it."

"I hope we have nice weather tomorrow," I spoke up, changing the subject. Noreen glanced over and shrugged.

"We're supposed to. But this is the Midwest. Just hang around for ten minutes, and the weather will change."

I was glad when she turned on the radio. I settled back against the seat and just watched the scenery go by the rest of the way to the cabin. I was surprised to see Jimmy Frank's truck waiting for us there. An old beat-up Chevy was parked beside the steps, and there were folding tables and lawn chairs strapped across its top.

"What took you so long?" Tyler greeted us, propped lazily in the doorway. "We're starved!"

"So what do you want *us* to do about it?" Noreen faked surprise.

"Don't tell me you didn't bring anything to eat tonight." Tyler groaned. "I can't work on an empty stomach!"

"The secret to being popular," Noreen confided to me in a smug whisper as she went around to the trunk, "is to always bring the food!"

Behind Tyler, Jimmy Frank was watching us get out of the car. His arms were crossed over his chest, and as Noreen waved, he threw her a glance that was almost indifferent. I could feel him staring at me, and I tried to ignore him as I helped Noreen unload her car. Then I went inside with Dobkin while Tyler showed him around.

The time passed quickly. For all my earlier uneasiness, I had a really good time, and the best part of all was that I didn't think about Suellen once. As the evening wore on, even Jimmy Frank seemed a little more relaxed, smiling at Tyler's dumb jokes, answering Dobkin's questions about what it was like to live on a farm. The four of us scrubbed the cabin from top to bottom while Dobkin divided his attention between watching TV and playing in the back of Jimmy Frank's pickup. For our dinner break Tyler grilled steaks outside, while Noreen and I made a huge salad, and Jimmy Frank took Dobkin for a walk. The two of them came back half an hour later with rocks and a snakeskin and a huge turtle, which Dobkin informed me he was taking home as a pet.

I turned to Jimmy Frank to thank him. He was leaning back against the wall watching Dobkin with this kind of half-tolerant, half-amused look on his face, and Dobkin was telling me how Jimmy Frank was going to take him fishing.

"He knows this secret place on the river," Dobkin informed me, about as excited as I'd ever seen him. "He promised he'd take me there sometime."

I stared at Jimmy Frank, and his eyes shifted slowly onto mine. He looked like he was almost smiling, yet there was still this wariness about him, this holding back.

"Thanks," I said. "I guess you know you've made a friend for life."

He didn't say anything. He shrugged and glanced briefly at Dobkin, and then he went outside, where Tyler was busy with the steaks.

It was late by the time we were ready to leave. The cabin looked great, and as we all went out to our cars, we made plans about what time to meet the next day. I felt warm and happy inside, watching everyone say good night. There was this sense of accomplishment about the cabin, and this sense of camaraderie I'd missed out on for so long, and as I watched Tyler and Noreen laughing and teasing each other, I found myself thinking that maybe—finally—this was a place I could end up belonging.

"Marlee, come on!" Noreen's voice jarred me out of my reverie, and I realized that the others were getting into their cars.

"I'll take her home," Tyler said. Noreen and Jimmy Frank exchanged looks, and he drew himself up indignantly. "Oh, what? What's the big deal? I mean—I *do* live right next door to her!"

"We know," Noreen cooed sweetly.

"I'm only being sensible about this," Tyler went on. "I'm only thinking about you. So you won't have to go out of your way."

Noreen was smiling and nodding her head. "I know, Tyler. And don't think for a second that I don't appreciate your unselfishness. Your kindness. Your chivalry."

"I want to ride with Jimmy Frank," Dobkin spoke up. "He said I could go in the back of the truck."

I started to protest, but Jimmy Frank already had ahold of him, lifting him onto the bed of the pickup.

"It'll be okay," he assured me. "I'll drive slow till we get to town, and then I'll put him back inside."

"Well, good night, all." Noreen waved, stifling a yawn. "See you guys tomorrow. Marlee—is nine too early for grocery shopping?"

"No—see you then." I waved back.

Tyler and I got in his car and led the procession out. We crossed the bridge and stopped to put the chain back up. Noreen passed us, honking her horn. Jimmy Frank pulled around us, too, and I caught a glimpse of Dobkin squeezed back into one corner of the truck bed. He was wearing Jimmy Frank's hat.

"Tired?" Tyler asked as we started off again.

"Exhausted," I admitted. I looked over and smiled at him. "It was fun, though. I had a really good time."

"I'll remember that after the party tomorrow," Tyler said, straight-faced. "When it has to be cleaned all over again."

His hand slid across the seat and lightly covered my fingers.

"Why don't you close your eyes?" he said softly. "It'll be a while till we get home. You can take a nap, if you want."

The thought was tempting. Darkness flowed thickly past the car windows, and Tyler's hand stroked mine, and suddenly I could hardly stay awake.

"I should watch out for Dobkin," I murmured.

"Why?" Tyler asked. "He's with Jimmy Frank, and they're way ahead of us by now. He'll be okay."

My eyelids drooped. I leaned my head back against the seat, and I let myself drift.

The explosion shattered my sleep.

Bolting up, I looked around in confusion, trying to remember where I was, and then I saw Tyler beside me, leaning partway out his open window.

"Damn," he muttered, "we've got a flat."

He pulled the car off to the shoulder beneath some trees. As I sat there shaking and trying to come fully awake, I stared out at the pitch-black road and felt a sudden stab of fear. The woods were swarming with shadows. The silence was unnerving . . . unnatural.

"Do you think the others know we're in trouble?" I asked Tyler as he opened his door.

"Of course they don't know," he informed me. "And we're not in trouble. I know how to fix a flat tire."

I couldn't stay there in the car alone. I climbed out after Tyler and glanced around nervously at the darkness. Suddenly I was frightened—really frightened— with this strange, deep knowing inside me that something horrible was about to happen.

"Damn!" Tyler said.

"What is it?"

He was squatting beside the left front tire. He had a flashlight in his hand, and he swung it angrily against the side of his car.

"This is crazy," he muttered. "It looks like the tire's been cut."

He went around to the back. I heard him open the trunk and rummage around. In a few seconds he came back with a tire iron and squatted down again.

"Can I help?" I asked him.

"Sure. You can hold the light while I try to get this stupid thing off."

He pried at the hubcap, popping it free. He swore again under his breath.

"Now what?" I worried.

"The lug wrench." He sighed. "Would you mind?"

I shook my head and started around to the trunk.

I shone the flashlight into the dark interior, and I leaned slowly forward, groping through a clutter of old tools, trying to find the one he needed.

And then I froze.

My hand stopped in midair and my blood stopped in my veins and my heart stopped beating while the whole world slammed to a sickening halt—

"What is it, Marlee?" a voice said softly in my ear.

I spun around, my mouth open to scream, and Tyler was right there, his eyes narrowed, taking a step toward me, reaching out his hands—

"No," I whispered. "Oh, no . . . no . . ."

"What?" His voice was low . . . only a whisper now, and he was coming closer . . . closer . . . "What is it, Marlee . . . what do you see . . . ?"

"She was here!" I cried, and the silence shattered around me, but not the picture I could see in my mind—the horrible vivid picture in all its gory detail—

"What are you talking about?" he mumbled.

He took another step. I crouched back against the fender and stared at him, and then I glanced wildly into the yawning hole of the trunk—

"Suellen!" I screamed. "She was here! Right inside here! *Right before she died!*"

I saw Tyler's arm lifting at his side.

I saw the tire iron clutched in his hand.

And I saw the trees reaching out to catch me as I plunged into the woods and ran.

23

Marlee! Marlee, come back here!"

His voice followed me through the night.

I didn't know where I was going, I only ran, ran for my life, and tried to escape—from Tyler, from Suellen, from the grisly pictures in my mind.

She was lying there . . . stuffed inside the trunk . . . blood on her face . . . wet and muddy . . . lying there with her eyes closed and—

"Marlee! Where are you!"

He was getting closer.

With a ragged sob I fought my way through the trees, slipping, falling, staggering up again, on again.

He'll leave me in here—here in these woods—and no one will ever find me again—just like they'll never find Suellen—because I'll be dead, too, and I'm the only one who knows—

"Marlee!"

"Oh, God, no—"

I didn't see the gaping hole in front of me.

In the terrifying darkness I didn't see how the ground suddenly dropped off and disappeared—not till it was too late and I was tumbling headfirst down the hill. For several seconds I lay there, too stunned to move, but my will forced me up again, and I turned in helpless circles, trying to get my bearings, trying to find my way out.

Moonlight trickled down into the ravine.

I thought I saw a break through the trees, and I stumbled toward it.

"No, Marlee," Tyler said behind me. "You're not going anywhere."

I screamed, and then I screamed again. He clamped one hand over my mouth and jerked me backward, pressing me tight against him so I couldn't move.

"Stop it!" he hissed. "What the hell is the *matter* with you!" He spun me around to face him.

She was lying there in the trunk . . . but she was still breathing . . . She looked like she was dead . . . but . . . she was still alive—

"Marlee!"

He was shaking me—hard. I flopped like a rag doll in his grip, and I looked up into his face, and there were scratches over his cheeks and blood on his forehead, and his eyes were gleaming and wild—

"What's the matter with you, dammit? What's going—"

"You killed her!" I screamed then, my voice shrill with hysteria. I saw the dark pools of his eyes and the open circle of his mouth. "She was in your trunk! She looked like she was dead, but she was still alive! What did you do with her? Where did you take her!"

"My God," Tyler murmured.

I felt his hands slide down my arms. He took a step away from me, and he stumbled, dropping something onto the ground. For one long moment he stared down at the tire iron, and then he ran one hand slowly through his hair.

"You—" He was having trouble talking. His words sounded choked and tight. "You—think—that I—"

"I *saw* her, Tyler! Suellen was in your trunk just before she died! You hurt her, and then you took her somewhere else to kill her! Where is she, Tyler! *Where!*"

But he was still staring at me, and his eyes were wild in the moonlight, and his face was drained white, and he kept stepping back, stepping back . . .

"My car?" he repeated numbly. *"My* car?"

My eyes filled up. I stared at him through a mist of tears and felt my heart breaking.

"Oh, Tyler," I whispered. "Why did you do it?"

His legs seemed to give out then; he sat down hard on the ground. He lowered his head between his hands. It took several minutes for him to look up at me.

"Marlee," he said slowly, but his voice was strong again—strong and calm and even. "Marlee, I didn't even have my car that day."

Roaring . . . roaring and rushing through my head . . .

"What . . . what did you say?" I mumbled.

"I was out of town when Suellen disappeared. I was with my folks that weekend, and we were out of town. I didn't even use my car."

My eyes never left his face. He looked beaten and exhausted . . .

And hurt.

"You thought . . ." He took a deep breath. "You thought . . ."

"Who had your car that weekend, Tyler?" I mumbled.

His face looked strained. He looked like he was trying not to cry.

"Hey!" a voice shouted through the woods. "Tyler! Marlee! Where are you guys?"

Tyler leapt to his feet.

I felt his arms go around me and yank me back against him as something crashed through the trees and underbrush down the side of the hill.

"Come on, you two!" another voice yelled. "Are you okay? Why don't you answer!"

I could feel Tyler's heart against my back. It was pounding out of control.

"Shit," he whispered.

The next minute two faces broke through the shadows, ghostly and deathly white in the glow of a lantern.

"There you are!" the first voice called. "Thank God!"

But I couldn't answer.

I couldn't speak . . . I couldn't even move.

All I could do was stare as that lantern swung high

in the darkness, stare at the face of the person who held it.

I saw the familiar features . . . features hideously distorted now by the pale, hazy lantern light . . .

And I knew then what Suellen had seen in the very last second before she died.

24

You!" I gasped, and the night spun around me, sick and dizzy and twisted. *"You* killed her!"

Jimmy Frank lifted the lantern high beside his head. His eyes glittered fiendishly, and his smile was like ice. I was hardly even conscious of Tyler stepping in front of me.

"What are you talking about, Marlee?" Jimmy Frank said calmly. "You must be hallucinating again."

But I wasn't listening to him—didn't hear him— my mind was spinning so fast, I felt sick to my stomach, images—feelings—slamming me from every side—and I clutched my head, trying to hang on to my sanity.

"You killed her," I choked, "you *killed* her—"

"Oh, for Christ's sake." Jimmy Frank sighed. "Do we have to stand here and listen to this all night? I don't know what the hell she's—"

"She was in the car"—I was babbling now and couldn't stop—"in the car, with her eyes closed. But—but she wasn't dead. Not yet—"

They were all staring at me. Noreen's mouth had dropped open and her arms were up, as though she could somehow stop the flow of words gushing out of me. I could see her, but it didn't make any difference —the pictures were flashing so fast, so furious in my mind, that I couldn't have stopped them no matter what I did.

"She wasn't dead—she only *seemed* dead because she wasn't moving. You took her somewhere—dark . . . cold . . . I see her lying there with her eyes shut. I see her lying there, and something's falling on her. Rain? Snow? No . . . dirt! Dirt and rocks and mud! Someone's—someone's throwing them—there's a shovel—"

"Jimmy Frank," Noreen whimpered, and he turned on her.

"Shut up!" he raged. "Just shut up!"

"A shovel," I raced on, my throat tightening, my blood pumping furiously as my heart screamed and screamed—*Suellen's terror*—*Suellen's pain*— *Suellen's aloneness*—

"She was lying there, and the dirt was falling . . . my God . . . my God . . ."

"Jimmy Frank, you promised!" Noreen shrieked.

"Shut up!" he yelled again.

"You put her somewhere—" I grabbed my stomach, trying not to be sick. "You thought she was dead . . . you thought she was dead, but she wasn't. . . ."

Even in the lantern light I could see the color draining from Jimmy Frank's face. He clutched the lantern tightly and fell back a step as if he'd been hit.

"You're lying," he hissed. "She *was* dead—I checked her myself—there wasn't a pulse—"

"My God," I sobbed, "you *buried* her! She was still alive, and *you buried her!*"

"You're crazy!" He laughed, a hoarse, choked sound. "What—are you two really going to stand here and listen to this crap? I can't believe I'm hearing it! Some total outsider comes in and—"

"You were the last one she saw when she died!" I was sobbing now, sobbing and shouting at him. "It was *your* face she saw through the falling dirt, *your* face looking down at her as she clawed through the mud and panicked and struggled for air—"

"No!" Noreen shrieked. "You said you'd take care of it! You said *I* killed her—but—but—she wasn't even dead—"

"Noreen—" Jimmy Frank took a threatening step toward the girl, but she stood her ground, still screaming at him.

"You said you'd take care of it! You said I'd never have to worry about what happened!"

"Noreen," he snarled, "shut *up!*"

"You let me believe I did it!" she cried. "All this time—I thought I'd go crazy—you said she hit her head and she was dead! But you must have known she was still alive, and you let me believe I killed her—"

"Shut up!"

"It was an accident. . . ." Noreen was sobbing uncontrollably now. "I didn't mean to push her! I picked her up after school on my way to Tyler's cabin, and she told me she had proof that Jimmy Frank was breaking into the summer homes on the river! She threatened to tell on him—"

"Noreen—you're crazy!" Jimmy Frank shouted, but she rushed on.

"When we got to the cabin, I was so upset with her and I begged her not to tell on him, but she just laughed at me and started walking away! So I tried to grab her and make her stop, but she slipped and fell! She rolled down the hill and hit her head on the way down—and she was caught in the tree roots and hanging facedown in the water. . . ."

Noreen's voice trailed away. Her head lowered slowly to her chest, and when she finally spoke again, it was like she'd gone into some kind of a trance.

"I thought Suellen was dead. She wasn't moving . . . there was blood coming out of her nose . . . from her mouth . . ."

Noreen stopped. She took a deep shaky breath. Her whole body sagged, but still she didn't look up.

"Jimmy Frank showed up then—he was doing some work on the cabin. And when he got there and I told him what she'd threatened to say about him—"

"Don't listen to her," Jimmy Frank broke in. *"She's* the one who killed Suellen, not me. She pushed her down the hill! You heard her admit it! And then she hid the body so no one would ever know—"

"You swore!" Noreen's head snapped up, her voice trembling. "You swore you'd take care of it! 'Leave it to me, Noreen—no one will ever know what happened'—isn't that right? You knew Tyler was out of town and I was borrowing his car, so you had me drive *your* truck home, and you used Tyler's Chevy to take Suellen's body. You said it'd be easier to hide her in a trunk than in the back of the pickup—but really, you just wanted *Tyler* to look suspicious instead of you! And you said if anyone ever found out about the robberies, you'd fix it so Tyler would go to jail with the rest of us."

Tyler seemed dazed. He was staring at Noreen with this horrible look of pain on his face, and when he finally spoke, I could barely hear him.

"Noreen," he murmured. "Why didn't you tell me? Why didn't you—"

"Because I was *so scared!*" she screamed at him. "Because I wanted you to get the scholarship, and I didn't want anything to spoil it! This way you never knew—and even if anyone asked you, you wouldn't have had to lie!"

"Oh, Noreen," he whispered. "I'm so sorry. . . ."

And suddenly Noreen began to laugh. She grabbed fistfuls of hair in her hands, and she threw back her head, and she laughed and laughed. It was an unearthly sound, and I felt cold to my very soul.

"You said no one would ever find out!" She turned to Jimmy Frank, and she was gasping for breath, laughing . . . laughing . . . "And I really—*really*—thought you'd *have* to love me now, 'cause we were in this together! You never expected Marlee to come along—"

Jimmy Frank slapped her. She fell back from the blow, fixed him with a long, silent stare, and then crumpled to her knees.

"Oh, God," she whimpered, "what have I done. . . ."

Tyler started toward her when there was a sudden rustle in the underbrush. Jimmy Frank spun around, and to my horror, I saw Dobkin scramble out of the woods, his face desperate with fear.

"Marlee!" he yelled. "Marlee, where are you?"

"Dobkin!" I screamed. "Go back to the car! *Run!*"

I think somehow he knew, even before Tyler and I both lunged for him. I saw him bolt for the trees, but Jimmy Frank snatched him back before Dobkin had gone even two feet.

"Not so fast, little guy," Jimmy Frank said softly. "I've got plans for you."

I never saw where the gun came from.

One minute Dobkin was kicking and twisting, and the next he was frozen still with Jimmy Frank's pistol against his skull.

"Let him go!" I screamed. "He doesn't have anything to do with this!"

"On the contrary, he has quite a *lot* to do with this." Jimmy Frank gave a slow, chilling smile. "He has big eyes and big ears. They pick up things they shouldn't."

It all happened so fast.

I saw Dobkin's little legs flailing out at Jimmy Frank's shins, saw him bite down on Jimmy Frank's hand. And then there was a sickening thud, and Dobkin's body went limp in Jimmy Frank's arms.

"No!"

"You shouldn't have come here," Jimmy Frank spat at me. "You're an outsider, and you don't have any right to stick your nose where it doesn't belong—"

"Let him go!" I begged. "What have you done to him! He might be dying!"

I could see Dobkin dangling in Jimmy Frank's grip, and as Tyler made a move toward him, Jimmy Frank slammed the pistol once again to Dobkin's head.

Tyler stopped and threw me a frantic, helpless look.

"Coming here with your *feelings*—your *stories*— making people remember all over again! If you'd just taken the warning and left when you had the chance! If you'd only taken the warning—"

"It was you in my room that night!" It suddenly dawned on me. "You tried to scare me! And you put the roaches in my locker! You came into my room and hid under my bed—were you planning to kill me then?"

"Scare you," Noreen mumbled, and everyone jumped and looked at her where she still knelt on the ground.

"He wanted to scare you off. . . . He wanted me to help him." She stared at the ground and kept mumbling. "He realized your brother had taken his bandanna. He was afraid you'd be able to read things from it—the way you could from Suellen's locker. That you'd know *he* was the one who took care of Suellen. He watched your house all the time. It was easy with the empty lot behind it—and sometimes he even peeped in your windows. He even tried to convince Tyler that something was wrong with you— mentally—so Tyler could find out how much you really knew."

A faint smile touched her face.

"But that didn't work," she murmured. "'Cause

Tyler liked you too much. So then Jimmy Frank tried to pretend he was psychic, too. Thinking you'd confide in him and tell him what you'd figured out."

But I was hardly listening to Noreen anymore. I could only stare at Dobkin's limp little form hanging in Jimmy Frank's arms.

"Let him go, and we'll leave tonight," I begged. "I can *make* my aunt leave, if that's what you want. We'll go away, and we'll forget we ever heard of you or the town—just please don't hurt my brother."

"Hurt him?" Jimmy Frank mocked me. "I promised the kid a trip downriver. So that's where I'm gonna take him."

"No!" I cried, and Tyler took another step toward them.

"Don't be stupid, Jimmy Frank—you'll have to get rid of all of us now. You'll never be able to hide it—"

"Shut up, Tyler. There're plenty of accidents on Lost River—plenty of people who never come back. Kids go out there and get careless. Get lost. Fall down ravines and hit their heads. Fall out of boats and drown. Do you think I'm worried about that? I'm the sheriff's son. I'm the responsible caretaker. I'm the one everybody's gonna comfort when they find the bodies of my friends."

He smiled. In the flickering lantern light, his face was a hideous mask.

"The sheriff's son," he mumbled. "Who would ever have thought? And poor stupid Suellen Downing lying at the very bottom of our old well, right there on the farm. The well my dad had me fill in last winter 'cause he was afraid someone would have an accident."

Noreen's head came up slowly. "Jimmy Frank—"

"Shut up, Noreen. Get in the truck."

But Noreen was laughing again . . . quietly . . . to herself. Soft . . . satisfied . . . frighteningly resigned.

I never actually saw her leap for the gun.

One second she was on the ground beside Jimmy Frank—the next, she was struggling with him, screaming at the top of her lungs.

Tyler sprang forward with a yell, and from the hopeless tangle of bodies, I saw my little brother fall to the ground.

"Dobkin!"

I raced over to drag him to safety, and an agonized scream cut through the darkness.

I saw Tyler stumble backward, his hands on his head as he stared down at the ground.

"No," I whispered, "oh, no . . ."

Tyler turned and looked at me. He looked at me for a long, long time. And then he walked over and picked Dobkin up and gathered both of us into his arms.

"Don't," he murmured.

But I had to.

I had to see Noreen sitting there all alone, caught eerily in the lantern light, cradling Jimmy Frank in her lap.

There were pieces of his head splattered across her shirt.

She was covered with his blood, and as she slowly raised her eyes to us, she let the tire iron fall onto the wet, red ground.

25

"There he is again"—Dobkin shook his head solemnly—"sitting out in that tree."

Glancing up from my homework, I jumped off the bed and went to the window, opening it so I could lean out. I could see the branches all tangled together, and two legs hanging out of them, swinging.

"What are you doing?" I demanded.

"What does it look like I'm doing?" came the muffled reply.

"Get out of there."

"It's a free tree."

"Come inside. It's raining like crazy."

I glanced back at Dobkin, who was lying at the foot of my bed with his turtle. His arm was still in a cast, and the bump was still on his head, and all the scratches hadn't quite healed yet on his face, but Dobkin is a kid who's proud of battle scars.

"Come on out," Tyler said.

"I will not. It's cold out there."

Before I could back away, he was at the window with his arms around me, pulling me out on the limb, and in seconds I was soaked through.

Tyler looked at me with disgust.

"Ugh. You're all wet. Get away."

In response I threw my arms around his neck and kissed him, making sure I got him good and soaked. I pulled away, and that funny little smile played over his lips.

"You find me irresistible, don't you," he said.

"Don't flatter yourself."

"Truth is truth. Your life was empty without me."

"My life was sane without you."

"Same difference."

"Hmmm."

He grinned and shifted his body gracefully on the limb. He glanced over and his voice got serious.

"I hear things might go pretty well for Noreen."

"Really? Oh, I hope so. . . ."

"She's got a good lawyer. He's reminding everybody that she really *wasn't* the one who killed Suellen, and that she *was* the one who saved our lives."

"Do you think she'll ever come back here?"

"To Edison?" He shook his head. "No. Too many memories . . . too much talk. It's better for her— and her parents—to make a fresh start somewhere else."

"I'll miss her," I said.

"Yeah," he whispered. "Me, too."

I watched the pain and sadness go over his face, and I reached up to touch his cheek.

"She really loves you, you know."

A nod. "I know."

The silence stretched on. Only the raindrops and the distant rumble of thunder and Dobkin humming to himself inside my room.

"How about you?" Tyler finally asked.

"How about me what?"

"Loving me."

"Not a chance."

"You could do worse."

"And a whole lot better."

"I doubt it. I'm pretty cute."

"Who told you that?"

"You did."

I turned to him and tried to hide a smile, but he hugged me, and I smiled all over.

"I guess I was right," I said.

He nodded. "About most things."

I looked at him, and the last few weeks flooded through my mind, and suddenly it was almost hard to remember the fears and the pain . . . only the relief and the joy. My mind was wonderfully free now . . . I knew Suellen was finally at peace.

Still, I couldn't help leaning over and taking Tyler's hand. I held it up and squinted at it, and saw him watching me intently.

"What do you think you're doing?"

"I have this feeling . . ." I said.

"Which is?"

"That you're going to kiss me just about any second now."

Tyler's eyes went wide. He looked at me in amazement and slowly shook his head.

"Wow," he breathed. "You really *are* psychic."

And as he took me into his arms, the rain didn't matter at all.

About the Author

Richie Tankersley Cusick loves to read and write scary books. Richie enjoys writing when it is rainy and gloomy outside, and likes to have a spooky soundtrack playing in the background. She writes at a desk that originally belonged to a funeral director in the 1800s and that she believes is haunted. Halloween is one of her favorite holidays. She and her husband decorate the entire house, which includes having a body laid out in state in the parlor, life-size models of Frankenstein's monster, the figure of Death to keep watch, and scary costumes for Hannah and Meg, their dogs. A neighbor recently told them that a previous owner of the house was feared by all of the neighborhood kids and no one would go to the house on Halloween.

Richie is the author of *Vampire, Fatal Secrets, The Locker, The Mall, Silent Stalker, Help Wanted,* and the novelization of *Buffy, the Vampire Slayer,* in addition to several adult novels for Pocket Books. She and her husband, Rick, live outside Kansas City, where she is currently at work on her next young adult novel.